Private Property

There's nothing casual about this caper...

Jodi Tyler has loved and lost too many times to believe in happily ever after. That's what makes her no-strings affair with her boss so perfect—his power in bed matches his respect for her independence. Still, when he surprises her with a ménage for her birthday, her secret thrill wars with a nagging thought: Why would he so casually share her with another man?

Even though Mark Rodriguez holds Jodi at arm's length from his heart, her self-confidence is a turn-on he can't resist. Inviting old college buddy and future business partner Sam into their bed for one night was supposed to set free her wildest fantasy. Instead he finds the tables turned, forced to watch while Sam brings her to the height of ecstasy.

Now, Mark's not so sure he wants to share his treasure...

Warning: This book contains a woman fulfilling her sexual fantasies—including two men who are happy to tie her up, and be tied up, while using graphic language and floggers.

Deliberate Deceptions

A little lying and misdirection in the name of love is never wrong. Right?

Chad Miller once had the perfect life—a beautiful baby daughter, a loving wife, a promising career with the FBI. Within a year, he'd lost everything. Making Hauberk Protection a success salvaged his career, but he's never managed to get over the one fateful decision that spelled the end of his marriage. And the death of his child.

For eight years, grief and guilt have haunted Lauren Miller's climb up the ranks of the Light Brigade, a secret international hostage rescue team. Now she's the target of a vengeful ex-Brigade operative who'll stop at nothing to take her down. Even if it means taking out everyone she cares about. Including Chad. Getting him to accept her as his bodyguard? It'll take some fast talking—and faster hands.

Trapped in a remote safe house with Lauren is the last place Chad ever wanted to be. He may finally have the chance to get some answers about why she ran, but with his hard-won defenses crumbling, he's having trouble remembering the questions. In the heat of their rekindled passion, Lauren struggles to keep her professional focus...and keep the secrets that could break his heart all over again.

Warning: Angst dead-ahead! Lost love. Angst. Reunited lovers. Angst. Sex. More angst. And did I mention the angst? A box of tissues is definitely needed. But don't worry, there's still a Happy-Ever-After.

Look for these titles by

Leah Braemel

Now Available:

Hauberk Protection

Private Property

Personal Protection

Deliberate Deceptions

Hidden Heat

Private Deceptions

Leah Braemel

Samhain Publishing, Ltd.
11821 Mason Montgomery Road, 4B
Cincinnati, OH 45249
www.samhainpublishing.com

Private Deceptions
Print ISBN: 978-1-61921-182-7

Editing by Tera Kleinfelter
Cover by Kendra Egert

Private Property, ISBN 978-1-60504-368-5
First Samhain Publishing, Ltd. electronic publication: January 2009
Deliberate Deceptions, ISBN 978-1-60928-457-2
First Samhain Publishing, Ltd. electronic publication: May 2011
First Samhain Publishing, Ltd. print publication: January 2013

Contents

Private Property

Dedication

To my husband and sons who told me to "go for it". Thank you for putting up with my endless discussions about writing and for answering my sometimes-obscure questions about how guys think. I love you all.

To Becky, critique partner and whip-cracker extraordinaire, who has been there from the start. You poked and prodded and nagged me to keep writing even when I was ready to give up. I wouldn't be here without you, my friend. Thank you.

To my two other critique partners. Terri and Martie, who have eagle eyes and sharp red pens that force me to keep on my toes when writing.

And to my editor, Angela James. How you manage the workload you have, I have no idea. I am in awe.

Chapter One

A deep reverberating thrum filled Jodi Tyler's chest and stroked the back of her throat with its raw promise of latent power. The unmistakable growl of a Harley. The sound bounced off the highwalled estate hugging the shores of Lake Arlington, then abruptly stopped.

She lifted the night vision binoculars and peered through the tinted windows of the surveillance van. Nothing. Deciding there was no threat from the road, she swiveled her chair back to the monitors. Her fingers flicked the switches controlling the surveillance cameras aimed at the estate. Images flashed across the monitor in rapid succession. They all showed the same thing. Nothing.

So where had the motorcycle gone?

"Must've turned off," she muttered to herself. She grabbed the black T-shirt she'd discarded earlier and blotted the sweat trickling down her neck.

Maybe the pimply teenager three doors up drove a Harley. More likely his mid-life-crisis-aged father, she thought, wiping the perspiration pooled between her breasts.

Being stuck in a stifling black van in Dallas during a heat wave was not her idea of excitement. Especially on her birthday. Which Mark had forgotten.

Or ignored.

After hinting for weeks about how she wanted to spend the night, starting with a romantic dinner at their favorite restaurant, after teasing him about the sexy negligee she'd bought, even after that stupid list of all the sexual fantasies she'd written for him, he'd still gone ahead and arranged for her to penetrate the estate tonight. Tonight!

"If he expects me to be in any sort of romantic mood when I get home, he's got rocks in his head." She plopped down in the chair with a huff. "He can sleep in his own bed tonight. Alone."

She switched the monitor back to the camera aimed at the Lexus parked in front of the five-car garage. If the assistant kept to her regular schedule—and that woman was punctual to a fault—the car would soon be cruising up the drive. Which meant Jodi'd be out of this Easy-Bake Oven and into the air-conditioned estate to finish this assignment. Then she could go home and shower. Alone.

An insidious thought slithered into her mind, puncturing her self-confidence with an icy-cold needle. *That's what he's planned all along—he's trying to dump you without actually having to say anything.*

No, she thought, shaking her head. Mark doesn't play games like that.

How do you know? the voice whispered. *Why else would he arrange for the estate to be penetrated today of all days? He's easing his way out of the affair by pissing you off, hoping you'll dump him first. And don't forget how he insisted either one of you could walk away at any point.*

She leaned back in the chair, her arms folded across her chest. Easing out of a relationship had to be better than being dumped by text message the way Todd had done. *"Let's just be friends."*

Friends, my ass.

Would it hurt less than it had when she'd found another woman's bra under Danny's bed and been forced to endure his long, stumbling explanation? *"She's softer, less demanding, you know?"*

Yeah, she knew.

Permanent scars etched her heart after Jace's less-than-flattering comments about her lack of femininity when she'd graduated from the police academy. More fool her, she'd actually quit the force trying to please that asshole and he'd still dumped her.

Maybe Mark's way of easing out of a relationship *was* better. Maybe it would hurt less. She rubbed the heel of her hand over the ache in her heart. Who was she kidding? Despite agreeing with Mark that the affair wouldn't be long term, she'd fallen in love with him anyway. If he was breaking up with her, she was soon going to feel like her skin had been stripped off layer by layer.

When a branch snapped behind the van, interrupting her pity fest, she grabbed her gun from the console and headed to the driver's seat. There was no way she was going to sit here as a witless target.

"Jodi? Open up, babe, it's me," Mark whispered through the back panel.

Excitement flared in her chest at the sound of his voice. When she realized her heart was racing just from hearing his voice, she silently cursed herself for acting like a bookworm with a serious crush on the quarterback.

"Jodi?" Mark said, a little louder this time. "You okay in there?"

She thumbed on the safety of her Sig Sauer and, after taking a deep breath, opened the door. A glance around showed no sign of his Humvee—he must have parked it farther down the road and walked up.

"You could have phoned to say you were coming in. I might have shot you." In the groin.

The van dipped when he stepped up into it. His six-foot-two-inch frame filling the narrow confines, he gently closed the door so it wouldn't give away their position. The dragon tattoo on his biceps flexed as he placed a knapsack on the console beside the surveillance equipment. Muscles rippled beneath the *Celada Security* logo emblazoned across the chest of his black T-shirt. Muscles she'd felt flex beneath her palms the night before.

Her fingers itched to run themselves through the thick crop of black hair in his Marine high-and-tight. Normally she didn't go for guys with short hair, but that glistening four-inch-wide pelt reminded her of a mink coat she wanted wrapped around her body. Between her legs.

Get over that desire real fast, she told her fingers. "You're late."

"Got stuck at the lawyers'. There—" He stopped as his eyes adjusted to the gloom, reminding her of what she was—or rather, wasn't—wearing.

Every cell in her body went on high alert, trembled with need and expectation as if he'd touched her wherever he looked.

His grin widened and his chocolate brown eyes glinted. "Is a sports bra and thong the latest fashion for surveillance?"

Jodi flipped him the bird while she searched for the T-shirt she'd discarded.

"It was hot. I stripped down. So bite me," she said, though without the rancor she'd intended.

"Anything you say, babe." He pulled her against him and nipped at her earlobe. "But I fully approve of your outfit. Think I should make it part of the dress code."

"Yeah, that'll go over real well." She attempted to maintain her anger. And failed. "Everyone's been dying to see Hector's fat ass in a thong."

When his hands cupped her breasts, Jodi melted into his touch. Magic fingers, she thought, as his thumbs brushed her taut nipples. Was this the last time he'd touch her like this? Or was it just her insecurity making her paranoid?

"Have I told you lately how beautiful you are?" he said, his breath hot on her neck.

The citrus fragrance of his aftershave, and the lack of his usual dark five-o'clock shadow told her he'd recently shaved. His fresh scent reminded her how grungy she felt having been cooped up in over one hundred degree heat all day. It took a charming—or incredibly obtuse—man to tell a woman whose hair clung in damp strands to her neck and probably smelled like the inside of a stable that she was beautiful.

Surely a man planning on dumping her wouldn't be acting like this. Or was he overcompensating?

"The assistant leave yet?" His tongue brushed over her earlobe, sending a shiver down her spine.

"Um..." She struggled to think under the onslaught of sensation. His tongue trailed down her neck, teeth nipped at that spot that made her need him inside her. What was it about him that made her knees turn to jelly and her insides to liquid heat?

"Babe? Did Ms. Janssen leave?"

She barely heard him repeat the question when his hand released her breast and moved lower. She forced one eye open and peered over his shoulder at the monitor, verifying the car hadn't moved.

"No, not yet. If she keeps to her usual schedule she should leave in ten minutes. I thought I heard an engine a few moments ago. You see anything on the way in?"

"Nope." He turned her away from the monitor and pushed aside the thin strip of her thong. His fingers—those broad, callused, *talented* fingers—stroked her vulva, sending streaks of pleasure deep inside.

She struggled to maintain focus the way he could. "Must have been... Oh, Mark, yes, right there."

Her legs opened wider under his murmured instructions, while her hands fumbled with the zipper in his blue jeans. Fingers were all very well, but when there was a cock willing and eager to penetrate her—and from the rock-hard erection beneath her palm, he was more than ready—there was no contest. She heard the rustle of canvas when he reached behind her, and she wondered what was in the knapsack that he needed at this precise moment.

"Got a present for you." His mouth covered hers, swallowing her squeak of surprise when something hard and cold touched her labia and pressed inward. "Something to keep you on your toes."

A moan left her when the object started vibrating inside her. He had to be kidding!

She reached down to remove the vibrating egg, only to have her wrist circled by his fingers, pulling her hand away.

"Oh no you don't. Leave it in until I take it out myself." An intense look filled his dark eyes, replacing the earlier amusement. He stepped back, all business, and picked up her black twill pants. "Better put these on. The assistant will be leaving soon. Don't forget you have to get through the gate right after she leaves."

"I know the plan." She tugged on her pants, doing her best

to ignore the overwhelming need the device was creating. "Do you seriously expect me to break into the house and crack a safe with this damned thing vibrating inside me?"

He flashed a six-megawatt grin. "Yup, I do."

Jodi stuck her tongue out at him. Okay, it was childish, but she hated that he'd got her so hot and bothered and then wouldn't let her come. Until she noticed the bulge in his pants. Proving that despite Mark's business-like demeanor, he was just as horny.

"We've got a few minutes before Ms. Janssen leaves." She trailed a finger down his chest, slid her hand between them and rubbed his erection, intent on torturing him and silencing her insecurities. "You must be aching as bad as I am. No use both of us being unfulfilled all night."

His grin fading, Mark flipped a switch on the remote. The vibrations ceased within her, leaving her with a completely unsatisfied pussy. Damn it, she needed to finish what he'd started.

"Look, babe, I know you wanted to celebrate, but the owner insisted it be today. And since you're our best at infiltration..." He tucked the remote into his shirt pocket then lifted her hands in his.

At least he'd remembered her birthday.

When he pressed his lips against her knuckles, her insecurity crawled back under its rock. Hopefully forever.

"I'd still rather have you inside me than this vibrator."

He chuckled and kissed her fingers again. "I know. So would I. But we don't have time."

"So why are you insisting I keep it in?"

He let her hands drop and cradled her head to his shoulder briefly. "Just for fun. Besides, you're always practicing cracking those safes wearing headphones, listening to loud music and street sounds. So think of my present as just another distraction, something to add to the challenge."

She relented. A little. There were worse ways to be distracted—like having firecrackers or guns aimed at you—both of which had been done to her in the past. His professionalism had attracted her to him in the first place; it wasn't right that she snark about it now, she supposed. Besides, what could be more exciting than breaking into a house, knowing you could get caught, a vibrator your lover had placed deep inside arousing every fiber of your being? By night's end, she'd be so horny, so desperate for him, he could fuck her in the middle of Dealey Plaza at high noon and she wouldn't deny him.

She bent over to pick up her T-shirt, making sure Mark had a really good look at her butt. Might as well give him something to think about while she was away.

"You got the letter I'm supposed to leave in the safe?" The shirt muffled her voice as she pulled it over her head.

He held up a sealed envelope. "Right here."

She grabbed the envelope and shoved it in her pocket. "You sure the owner hasn't upgraded the system? Or tipped the current security company off?"

"Nah, I have his word that if you crack the safe tonight, I'll have a signature on a contract at our lunch tomorrow. And then I can concentrate on the merger." Mark perched on the edge of the console and folded his arms. A smug look on his face told her he expected her to encounter no problems.

Yet for all his confidence in her, the envelope weighed a ton in her pocket. "Mark, are you sure you want to sell out? You've worked so hard making Celada the top security firm in Texas—you can't just hand over the reins to some stranger, even if he was your old college buddy. You love running your own company too much to see it gobbled up by Hauberk Security."

He grabbed her hand and tugged until she stood between his legs. "It's just a merger, babe, not a complete takeover. I've told you I'll continue to run ops this side of the Mississippi, and Sam will manage everything to the east from D.C. We'll both have to agree on any major decision, each with an equal say."

"And if you can't agree?"

"It'll work out. Trust me." His hand cupped her buttock and squeezed as he glanced at the monitor behind her. "Time to move, babe. Ms. Janssen is driving toward the gate."

He couldn't have staged a better way to avoid the subject if he'd planned it.

After pulling on a pair of surgical gloves, Jodi picked up the two-way headset and tucked it around her ear. "Give me a sound check, will you?"

Mark flipped on the microphone to the radio, and whispered something in Spanish.

Shivers flared down her spine and sent a bolt of heat into her core. "One of these days I'm going to take Spanish lessons. What did you say this time?"

"I promised to tie your hands behind your back and make you get on your knees. Then I said I'm going to put my dick in your mouth until I spew come down your throat."

Grabbing the back-door latch, Jodi pressed her knees together as her pussy clamped around the egg lodged high inside. "If you'd let Javier do this job the way I'd suggested, I'd be on my knees in a heartbeat. But since you didn't, I guess you'll have to keep dreaming."

"Maybe. Maybe not." He winked and tossed her a black knit cap. "Forget something?"

With a muttered curse about wool caps and Texas heat,

Jodi tucked her hair beneath the cap's edges. Once Mark had flicked off the van's dome light, she eased the door open. As she squeezed through the narrow opening, branches scraped against the door's paint job and tugged at her thin black cotton shirt.

Headlights slanted up the curving driveway, backlighting the ornate wrought-iron gates that creaked as they swung open.

"Right on time. Someone needs to teach you there's safety in unpredictability, lady," she murmured.

The sleek dark blue Lexus drove through the gates and turned right.

"Show time, babe," Mark said over the headset.

Heart thumping, Jodi slid in through the gates as the motor whirred, jumping only slightly when the gate clicked shut behind her.

Keeping to the shadows cast by the half-moon, Jodi crept down the long driveway toward the sprawling three-story Tudor mansion. She skirted the massive garage, then followed the path around back and stopped by the first French door. Whatever security expert designed the current system hadn't insisted that a deadbolt be installed on this one. Or the installers had missed it. And that was the reason she—no, she reminded herself, Mark's company—was going to prove they were the best security firm in Texas.

She pulled out the thin strip of plastic she had tucked in the pouch on her belt and shoved it between the jamb and the latch. Seconds later, she straightened and opened the door.

As she'd expected, a red light flashed in the security panel beside the door. She punched in the number she'd memorized and breathed a sigh of relief when the light turned a steady green. They hadn't changed the security code since she'd reconnoitered. Another point for her report.

"I'm in," she whispered, knowing Mark was listening in the van. She wiped the sweat from the back of her neck, angling her head to catch the cool breeze rushing through the air-conditioning vent.

"You never told me how you got the security code," she heard Mark say in the earpiece as she headed through the empty room toward the center hallway.

"I have my secrets," she taunted. That weekend she'd bribed a maid to call in sick so she could fill in had paid off—even if it meant she'd had to scrub toilets. The work hadn't really been hard—the new owner had only furnished four rooms so far, so there'd not been much to clean.

A smile tugging at her lips, Jodi paused at the door to the office, ensuring it was empty. Moonlight streamed between the heavy curtains that flanked the French doors and across the floor in a rectangular pattern, slanting up the bookcases lining the walls. The red power light on the cordless phone reflected in the brass base of the banker's lamp on the desk. Assured she was alone, she walked confidently toward the desk.

"The safe's in the floor behind the desk," Mark reminded her. "Figure you've got less than an hour to crack the safe, leave the envelope and get out before the next patrol cruises by."

She rolled her eyes. Cruise was right—that's all the minimum-wage cop wannabees currently providing security did for their visual inspection. Her van had been parked in the area for a week now and they hadn't slowed down enough to read her license plate or check why she was there.

She pushed the leather office chair aside and knelt on the hardwood floor, inhaling a whiff of lemon furniture polish. The very same polish she'd applied on the weekend. Reaching beneath the desk, her fingers found the latch that would free the panel hiding the safe. Her breath left her with a whoosh when she heard the audible click.

"Got it!" she whispered, pumping her fist in the air. Now the real fun began.

Still on her knees, she reached down and swung open the square section of floor concealing the safe. A chuckle escaped her. She'd never bothered to tell Mark that during her stint as a replacement maid, she'd been assigned to dust this room. Or that she'd discovered the safe's combination on the flip side of the leather blotter.

"Hey, Mark, start the timer—I'll bet I can have this baby cracked in under three minutes."

Mark's low chuckle reverberated in her ear. "Two. Loser gets tied up and spanked."

Jodi's butt tightened. Spanking usually meant Mark was in the mood for ass play. Maybe she should deliberately take four minutes. No, she thought with wicked delight as she glanced at her latex covered fingers, it was time Mark got a taste of his own medicine.

"Then drop your pants, big boy, and show me your sweet ass, 'cause you're going to get a whoopin' tonight."

Clenching her penlight between her teeth, she leaned over the dial of the old-fashioned safe. Then jumped when the egg started to vibrate deep inside her.

Sonuvabitch. She stopped herself from screeching. She'd completely forgotten the damned thing. Her nipples hardened into swollen buds rubbing against her cotton T-shirt while her pussy throbbed in time with the vibrations.

No way was she going to let Mark win this bet. Ignoring the vibrator as best she could, she carefully turned the dial clockwise to the first number. Heard the click as the mechanism released. One-and-a-half-turns counterclockwise. Another click. Clockwise again. Click. Grinning, she checked her watch.

"Mark, your ass is going to be sore tomorrow," she whispered.

A quick tug on the handle opened the safe. Her penlight's thin beam of light illuminated a thick rope of gold with a massive ruby pendant resting upon a black velvet-covered board. A set of dangly earrings that matched the pendant and several diamond-encrusted bracelets winked back at her. A fortune in easily fenced gems and the idiot had left the combination to the safe where anyone could find it.

Shaking her head at the owner's stupidity, she pulled out the envelope. Then froze when the sliver of light from the French door lengthened, slid beneath the desk and over the safe.

She peered beneath the knee space under the desk. The moonlight outlined the shape of a dark figure shutting the doors.

"Under two minutes, Mark, I win," she announced as she crawled from beneath the desk. She straightened and smiled, expecting Mark to flash that sexy smile of his. She was so ready to fuck him, to have him ram his cock deep into her.

But her smile froze when the intruder took a step into the room and the moonlight gleamed off his head. His *shaved* head.

Not Mark.

"Welcome to my parlor, said the spider to the fly."

Chapter Two

A sudden blaze of light blinded her. Halogen lights glared on the open safe, on the desk. On her.

On him.

A good four inches taller than Mark, the intruder must have weighed at least fifty pounds more, every ounce pure muscle. He looked like he'd stepped out of the Matrix in a dark silk shirt that outlined every bulging muscle in his massive shoulders. While his shaved head gleamed, a day's worth of stubble shadowed his heavy jaw. Beneath thick dark brows and darker eyes, his nose had a slightly off-center look as if it had been broken several times. Leather pants clung like a second skin, accentuating the bulging package at the juncture of his legs. Everything about him screamed strength and power.

"If you're fixin' to tell me you're doin' some window-shoppin', this store is closed." He spoke in a slow southern drawl, nothing like Mark's sexy accent.

Her heart rate skyrocketed to triple digits as adrenaline catapulted through her system; sweat slickened the inside of her gloves. Why hadn't Mark warned her that someone was on the grounds?

"You're trespassin' on private property, sweet pea." His deep voice resonated through her chest, its slow cadence drumming a prisoner to the gallows.

Confidence wrapped itself around him in a comfortable cloak. Something in the way he held himself told her not to let his casual pose deceive her. He looked like he could have played defensive end for the NFL and would relish the opportunity to tackle her.

Jodi stared at the inky darkness behind him, hoping he hadn't brought backup. When no one else appeared, her heart rate decreased. Slightly.

"You the owner?" she asked, pleased that her voice didn't betray her anxiety. Or the fact that her pussy was throbbing from the egg still vibrating deep inside her.

"If you belonged here, sweet pea, you'd know who the owner was."

Did that mean he *was*? Or he wasn't?

She'd checked the names of the cleaning staff personally but couldn't remember anyone of his age or description. The property had been registered under a numbered corporation, and while Mark had met with the owner in person, he hadn't mentioned the man—or woman's name, Jodi amended to be fair.

Jodi lifted her chin, forced her voice to remain steady. "I'm with Celada Security. We've been approached about upgrading the security on this place. Part of the proposal included an agreement that we would breach the perimeter. So here I am—living proof of how pathetic the current system is."

She pulled the envelope from her pocket and held it out, along with her identification. "Here, this'll prove what I'm saying is true."

Goliath plucked the envelope from her hand and tossed it on the desk. "Anyone could have written that letter, sweet pea. It don't prove a damned thing."

He reached into his pocket. Oh my God, he was armed! And

she'd left her gun in the van. How could she have been so stupid?

Her mouth pulled a Sahara Desert as her gaze darted toward the door. It couldn't be more than four feet away. She could make it through and be halfway down the hall while he was still rounding the desk. If she could find some way to stop him following her, she might have a better chance of escaping. She inched closer to the doorway, trying hard not to be obvious.

"Ah, now, don't make me chase you. I may be big, but I'm fast." Instead of the knife or gun she was expecting, he pulled out a fat cigar and stuck it in his mouth, held a match to it. "And I guarantee I'll enjoy catchin' you."

An icy lump settled into her stomach as she realized that she still hadn't heard Mark respond. She eyed the door again, judging her chances, then glanced at the desk seeking a letter opener or something she could use as a weapon. Maybe a solid thump to his head with the brass banker's lamp would slow him down.

"Relax, sweet pea, I'm not goin' to hurt you." Smoke wreathed his head as he drew on the cigar then carefully placed the cigar in the ashtray beside the lamp. "Much."

Trying to anticipate what his next move might be, Jodi watched him like a mouse eyed a cat. A really hungry cat.

Before she had time to get away, he'd rounded the desk in a graceful move that belied his size. He crowded her against the wall, his body a furnace wrapped in leather and silk.

She craned her neck up to meet his gaze, and revised her approximation of his height. He had to be at least six foot five. But she'd been right about him being pure muscle.

"Dangerous business, breakin' into private property. Even more dangerous when it's mine."

Mine? Jodi narrowed her eyes. He *was* the owner? So why

didn't he just acknowledge that he'd hired the firm to expose the estate's weak spots? What was his game?

"You get a rush breakin' into other people's places, sweet pea? Thwarting their security?"

He grabbed her hand and held it flat against his groin. Against the enormous hard-on straining the buttoned fly. "Do you feel what capturing a trespasser does for me?"

His gaze flicked down her body as his grin widened. "You're a little skinny for my tastes but I'll bet you're a real wildcat in bed. We're gonna have a lot of fun tonight, we are. I can't wait to bury my cock in your sweet pussy." He dipped his head until his mouth was beside her ear and whispered, "I'll bet you're already dripping wet, aren't you?"

She snatched her hand away and dragged in a breath, forcing air into her too-tight lungs as she memorized his features. "It'll be a cold day in hell before that happens, asshole. Now back off before I shove your dick down your throat."

His lips twitching as if he wanted to laugh, he took a half step back, but not enough for her to sidle past him. "I'd rather shove it down yours."

"Just read the letter. It'll prove I'm who I say I am, and am doing what we were hired to do. Or if you don't believe the letter is legit, call Mr. Rodriguez yourself."

She rattled off Mark's cell phone number while wondering why he still hadn't responded over the headset.

When he unfolded the paper and started reading it, his eyebrows arched and his lips compressed into a controlled smirk.

"*My Sexual Fantasies.*" His eyes flickered up and he grinned while Jodi narrowed her eyes, trying to figure his game. "Sounds like an interesting letter your boss wrote, sweet pea."

Just what she needed—a smart-ass.

"Just read the damned thing," she ground out.

"I *am* reading." He unfolded the paper again. "My Sexual Fantasies. One, to try anal sex. Two, I want to be fucked by Mark while tied up and blindfol—"

What the hell? Jodi snatched the paper from him with a gasp and stared in horror at the list she had jokingly made for Mark.

"This is a mistake," she stammered. "It was supposed to be the letter Mark—I mean Mr. Rodriguez had written explaining exactly how we'd breached security and his recommendations to make the estate safer."

He chuckled and looked over his shoulder to the French doors. "Is that what it was supposed to say, *Mr. Rodriguez*?"

Jodi followed his gaze. The knapsack at his feet, Mark leaned against the doorframe, thumbs tucked into the belt of his jeans that rode low over his hips.

Tension drained like a plug had been pulled, Jodi sagged against the wall. Until she realized Mark was not out of breath, nor was he treating the other man with caution. In fact, he was downright relaxed and smiling. She straightened, vowing vengeance for his screwup with the list. And for not letting her know he was all right. *And* for not warning her someone was about to walk in on her. Not to mention the vibrator still buzzing away deep inside, driving her insane.

"Will you please explain that I work for you, *Mr. Rodriguez?*" she gritted out, her hands curled into fists. "And will you please turn *it* off?"

"Sam?" Mark arched an eyebrow at her captor.

"I'd rather leave it on," Sam grumbled, but he reached into his pocket and the vibrator immediately ceased.

"*You* had the...?" Jodi spluttered when he held the remote up for her to see. "But Mark had... Mark, what the hell is going on here?"

"Jodi Tyler, I'd like you to meet Sam Watson."

Sam Watson? *As in the owner of Hauberk Security and Mark's college buddy*? Jodi closed her mouth when she realized her jaw was hanging open. Was this some sort of joke?

"So is this really your place, or are you checking me out to make sure I meet your company's qualifications?"

"Yup, place is all mine." He smiled as he picked up the cigar, his gaze flicking over her again. "As for checking you out, there ain't a man alive who could fail to admire your...assets."

Annoyed at being held captive by the man who would soon be her new boss, she placed her hands flat on Sam's chest and pushed. And failed to budge him at all.

"Since you own one of the biggest security firms on the east coast, you obviously don't need Mark to upgrade your security—so why have me break in? Oh, and in case you haven't heard, there's a law about sexual harassment of employees. So you'd better have one damned good lawyer."

Sam's eyes widened; he quickly stepped back, letting Mark take his place.

"Relax, babe." Mark rubbed her shoulders in a move meant to pacify her but she batted them away.

Jodi shoved the paper in Mark's face. It was either that or kick him in the groin. "This list was supposed to be just between us. How could you humiliate me like this?"

Mark cleared his throat and cursed softly in Spanish. "I'm sorry, babe, I wanted to surprise you for your birthday—you know, so we can cross the rest of those items off your list. I thought it would be funny. Sort of an icebreaker. "

“Funny?” She thumped her fist into his shoulder. “You have a twisted sense of humor. Besides, what could possibly be on there that you’d need to show to a perfect stranger?”

Sam waved his cigar toward the paper that was now a crumpled ball in her fist. “You might wanna refresh your memory and read number six there, sweet pea. Ol’ Mark here’s asked me to help fulfill that particular fantasy.”

With a growing dread, she scanned the list, her eyes widening.

6. I’d like to have a ménage with Mark and another man that we could trust.

Chapter Three

A ménage? While she'd secretly fantasized about that particular scenario, she'd not realized she'd actually written it down, nor that Mark wouldn't consult her on who the third person might be.

Wait a minute! This whole thing had been a setup? From the first time Mark mentioned the owner's challenge to break through the current security, to how he'd manipulated the roster so she pulled the majority of the surveillance? And this morning, when she'd tried to finagle the evening off so they could spend her birthday together, he'd insisted she be the one in the van...that she be the one infiltrating the estate. It had all been a lie?

"So you've been planning this for...what? A month now?"

"Yup. Ever since you wrote that list." Mark wore a smug, satisfied smile, like the proverbial cat who'd captured the canary—and still had yellow feathers clinging to his mouth. "Fooled you, didn't I? Happy birthday, babe."

Letting out a small screech, Jodi tore the list into pieces and flung them in Mark's face. She ripped off her knit cap and clutched a hank of her still-sweaty hair, holding it out at right angles. "So you made me spend twelve hours cooped up in a van until I smell like I spent all day in a swamp and thought that would put me in the mood for sex? And not just sex, but for fucking my future boss?"

"Told you you might want to rethink the idea of just springin' it on her, ol' buddy," Sam murmured.

She continued as if she hadn't been interrupted, poking Mark in the chest with one finger. "Did you think I might not like to have a say in who is the third? Or that it might affect how *Mr. Watson* judges me in the future?"

"Two-way street, sweet pea. You don't need to worry about me judgin' you for your sexual preferences if you don't judge me. An' I told Mark I wasn't gonna participate unless you were willin'." Sam tamped the cigar out in the ashtray once more, his face a carefully blank mask. "Guess I got my answer. No harm, no foul."

"Sam, wait," Mark said, running a hand over his thick strip of hair. "Look, Jodi, maybe I should have let you in on it from the get-go, but if you remember when you wrote that list, I promised that I'd try to fulfill all your fantasies. That's what I am trying to do."

She attempted to resist him when he tugged her close, refusing to look at him. He wrapped his arms around her, cradling her until she melted against him.

"Babe, I trust Sam more than I'd trust any other man with you." He pulled back and looked at her with narrowed eyes. "Or did you have someone else in mind?"

"No," she sighed. "I can't think of someone else."

"Tell you what," Sam said. "Why don't you two take a couple minutes and discuss it without me around? Go on up to the master bedroom and use that whirlpool tub big enough for six, or take a shower or something while you make up your mind. You might remember it since you did such a good job cleaning it when you played maid on the weekend—*Bianca*."

Jodi winced at Sam's use of the fake name she'd used.

Mark folded his arms across his chest and raised one eyebrow. Though he was attempting to be stern, the edges of his lips twitched as if he were trying to stop smiling. "So that's how you found out the security code."

"Girl's gotta have some secrets," she muttered.

"I'll be back directly." Sam picked up his cigar and stuck it in his mouth. "If you decide to stay, pick up the phone and dial pound-one-two."

He stopped in the doorway and winked. "Oh, and *Bianca*? Call me if you need any help scrubbin' up. I'm real good with a loofah."

Mark closed the bathroom door behind them, watching as Jodi wandered over to the long cherrywood vanity and stood in front of the gold-tapped white marble sinks, her lips pursed. She'd been quiet while she'd led him out of the study and up the stairs. He noticed she hadn't taken him to the master bedroom with the massive tub Sam had mentioned. Obviously she still wasn't comfortable with the idea of Sam joining them.

He should have at least given her a choice of who should be the "other man". And he should have realized she'd have wanted to primp a bit before the main event. *Way to go, Rodriguez.*

"We don't have to have the threesome. Just say the word and we'll go home and I'll never mention the list again."

Frowning, Jodi pulled the headset from her ear and set it on the white marble counter, watching it spin as it settled into place. Her tongue darted out, licked her top lip before she looked up into the mirror and met his gaze. "I know you meant well..."

Mark hesitated before voicing a concern that had raised its ugly head when he'd seen her reaction to Sam reading her fantasies aloud. “Jodi? Those things on the list—the bondage, the anal sex? Were they really things you wanted to try? Or were they just things you thought would keep me happy?”

Color rose up her neck and into her cheeks. He wondered if she realized she was wringing her hands.

Her tongue slid across her full upper lip again. “Some of them were.”

“Which means some of them weren’t.” He crossed the room in three strides, tugged her by the hips until she rested against him. “Why did you feel you needed to put things on the list if you didn’t want to try them? You know I’d never force you to do something you didn’t want to do.”

“Well, some of them I didn’t know I wanted to do until we did them. Like you fucking my ass, but then...” One shoulder lifted as her chin went down along with her lids, and the pink in her cheeks brightened to deep red flags. “I liked it.”

Mark barked a laugh that echoed around the room. “Liked it? That’s an understatement. I thought the neighbors were going to call the cops that first time, you screamed so loud when you came.”

She wrapped her arms around his neck and tilted her head back up so he could finally see her eyes were filled with a mixture of embarrassment and mirth. “And the night you tied me up was a real turn-on too. I had no idea I was such a control freak and that letting go would be so enjoyable.”

Her answer let him relax slightly. Her headstrong intensity when she’d stood up to clients—and him on occasion when their opinions had differed—was something that had first attracted him to her. He wanted to savor the fierce passion that simmered beneath her cool exterior. Forever.

He kissed the tip of her nose as he reached down and tugged her T-shirt over her head. “You don’t have to decide right now. Think about it while you take your shower."

She stepped out of her pants, leaving her once again in her thong and bra. He shifted so he stood behind her and pulled her against him. He looked at the image of them in the mirror and wondered why she—one of the most beautiful and intelligent operatives he'd ever met—had chosen him. And why she'd agreed to his no-attachments stipulation. He marveled at how her hair seemed to glow in the vanity lights. At how her full lips, slightly parted, urged him to kiss her. And how the light skin of her breasts contrasted with the tanned skin of his forearm cradling them. His dick firmed at the memory of three nights before when he'd come between them.

Though she'd never said a word of complaint, he knew his sexual demands had challenged her. He'd hated the thought that she might have done things she hadn't wanted to simply to please him. Those idiots who she'd dated before had her convinced she wasn't desirable. Damned if he'd let her think he thought the same thing.

"Open your eyes, babe."

The lights caught the sheen filling her eyes as she met his gaze in the mirror.

"Do you see what I see?" When she shook her head and tried to look away, he dipped his head and placed his cheek against hers to force her to continue looking in the mirror. "I see a beautiful woman with hair that's as bright as sunshine and soft as silk. I see dark grey eyes filled with love that brings me to my knees every time you look at me. I see full lips that make me hard just thinking of them wrapped around my dick."

Her pink tongue darted out to lick her top lip and her hips swiveled, pressing his erection into the crack of her ass.

"And that tongue of yours drives me crazy when it licks my balls, and swirls along my shaft as you suck me deep into your throat until I can't hold my come back any longer."

He cupped her breast, his thumb rubbing her nipple until it hardened. "I see a beautiful woman, with breasts that beg to be kissed. I see nipples as ripe as berries that make me want to suckle from them all night long."

His hand drifted over the smooth planes of her stomach to the thin triangle of hair at the juncture of her legs. "Full, pouty lips down here, too."

Jodi chuckled. When his fingers pushed aside the thin fabric and stroked, her chuckles changed to moans.

"And between those sweet lips of yours, there's a passage that's so tight and responsive I swear I lose my mind every time my cock slides into you."

Her head fell back against his shoulder and her hips rotated, betraying her insatiable need. He slid his hand over her hip and clasped one of her tight cheeks. "You've got the most beautiful ass any man could hope to see. Let alone fuck."

She murmured something about it being too big so he caught her gaze in the mirror, held it.

"Stop putting yourself down. You're beautiful." He released her and lightly slapped her butt. "Now you have your shower and decide what you want to do tonight. No pressure, all right?"

When he began to step back, she stopped him, cupping his head with her palm, pulling him down so she could kiss him. Her lips slightly parted, they brushed against his in a soft promise that quickly turned so hot he would have sworn the mirrors should have been coated with steam.

"I may need some help washing my back," she whispered, her breath warm against his cheek.

Chapter Four

Wearing a fresh set of clothes Mark had stuffed into the backpack, Jodi trailed him into the study. The only light in the room was provided by the green-shaded bankers' lamp on the desk. The floor panel once again concealed the safe, and the pieces of the list she'd scattered had disappeared. Sam stood in the shadows, his back to the room, staring out the door.

When Mark cleared his throat, Sam turned and tilted his head. "Let me assure you again, Jodi, that whatever your decision is, it'll not change anything between us in the future, especially in the office. I don't want you to feel pressured into anything tonight. Plus tonight is a one-time-only offer. When you walk away, whether anything happens or not, we will never discuss it again. That clear?"

Thoughts bounced randomly in her brain like popcorn in hot oil. Was she so boring in bed that this was what Mark needed to get excited? Would he walk away completely if she turned him down? And if she didn't, what would he demand next? An orgy, with her the main attraction?

No. Mark had also said if she turned his offer down, he'd never discuss it again. Two men at the same time. Could she live with herself if she agreed to Mark's plan?

She glanced down at the bulge between Sam's legs. And that was when he *wasn't* aroused.

Could she live with herself if she *didn't* agree? Or would she forever regret passing up the opportunity?

"So can we help you check another fantasy off your list?" Mark asked.

He moved close enough that she could feel the heat radiating from him, could smell the last lingering scents of herself on his breath. "Picture it, babe. Two mouths, two tongues to lick your breasts, to lap at your sweet pussy. Four hands to hold you, caress you, pleasure you." He pressed her hand flat against his groin, letting her feel his arousal. "And two cocks at your command."

As she watched, the bulge at Sam's groin grew, straining the leather taut. Heat rushed through her, and her eyelids grew heavy at the imagined sensation of the two men kissing her breasts; her pussy pulsed at the idea of being watched fucking Mark. Or Mark watching her being fucked by Sam. She licked her lips, imagining herself taking his cock into her mouth while Mark rammed into her from behind.

"I think...I think I'd like to stay. But I want you both to agree that if I decide to stop, you will."

"Of course, sweet pea," Sam quickly agreed. "Pick a safe word and we'll stop whatever we're doing the moment you say it."

Excitement mixed with trepidation slithered under her skin like an electric current.

"My safe word is...broccoli."

Both men exhaled as if they'd been holding their breath.

"Broccoli it is," Sam said. "Now before we get started, I just need your assurance about a coupla things."

"What?"

"Do you trust Mark's choice in me as the third? Do you

trust that I'll not hurt you or use anything that happens tonight against either of you?"

Her shoulders relaxed. She answered quickly, "Yes, I trust Mark's judgment. I mean, I trust you won't hurt me."

"Good." Sam walked over to her and held out one hand, as the other reached behind his back.

Smiling, she extended hers, expecting him to shake on their agreement. He took it, then immediately clamped a leather restraint around her wrist with his other hand. She let out a squeak and jumped back only to run into Mark's hard chest.

Sam's brows drew together until they met in the middle. "You wimping out already? Or have you forgotten item two on your list?"

Item two? To be tied up. Yeah, to be tied up by *Mark*, she wanted to tell him. Her lips parted as she began to object, then she closed them firmly. No, she had the safe word. Let's see where this led. She squared her shoulders and looked him straight in the eye. Bring it on. "You just surprised me, that's all."

"Standard procedure to cuff a burglar," Sam said.

All her apprehension fled as she realized the nature of the game they were going to play.

He held up a second wrist cuff and tossed it to Mark. "Why don't you do the other one? There's a clasp on 'em so they'll snap together just like handcuffs."

Mark bound her left wrist then pulled her hands behind her and snapped the cuffs together. He pulled on her arms, ensuring she couldn't free herself and grunted in satisfaction. "I think you should pat her down. You know, to ensure she's not concealing any weapons?"

Wrapping one arm across her chest, Mark held her firmly

against him. His breath blew hot in her ear, down her neck, sending a blast of heated blood through her belly to pool between her legs. While he'd often handcuffed her in private, she nearly whimpered in excitement at being held captive in front of a stranger. Her nipples hardened when his palm cupped her breast, squeezed. Hard. A moan escaped her, and she squirmed against the engorged length pressing into the cleft of her ass.

Her knees trembled as Sam's huge hands patted up her calves, her thighs, swept up her side, lingered over her breasts. He tweaked her nipples, and his lids drooped over his dark eyes.

"You broke into this place, you need to be punished. Don't you?"

"Yes," she whispered. "Punish me."

Chapter Five

A tornado whirled through her when Sam's large hand stroked her mound through the thin fabric of her pants, igniting fires in their wake. Jodi groaned, arched her hips into the broad fingers.

"She's so hot steam's risin' off her," Sam said with a chuckle.

From Mark's harsh breath beside her ear, and his rigid arm muscles, Jodi could tell he was not unaffected. The tension in his voice removed all doubt. "She likes relinquishing control. Most times."

Sam leaned down to her, the rough stubble of his beard scraping the tender skin of her cheek.

"Gorgeous." Sam stroked a strand of hair that curled over her ear. "It's like silk."

He stepped closer, ground his erection into her mound as he licked a spot just beneath her ear, the unexpected contact making her jump. Another moan escaped her at being sandwiched between the two aroused men. "Time for your punishment."

The leather of Sam's pants creaked as he pulled away from her and knelt in front of the credenza. He opened a cabinet door and removed a box, flipping open the lid. As he poked through it, Jodi strained to see what it contained, but Mark held her firmly in place.

Sam held up two thick leather collars, one encrusted with bright stainless steel spikes, the other glittering with what had to be rhinestones and rubies. There were so many they couldn't be the real thing. Could they? Besides who used real gems on bondage devices?

"Which do you prefer to restrain our suspect?"

Mark chose the spiked leather collar and carefully wrapped it around her neck.

Sam frowned. "We need a leash for that collar." He pulled out a silver chain and snapped the clasp over the ring on the collar. With a wide smile, he ceremoniously handed the chain to Mark. "Just to make sure she doesn't run away. Can't say we lost our suspect, now, can we?"

After rummaging through the box once more, Sam pulled out two matching anklets. Cool hands pushed her pants halfway up her calves, broad calloused fingers stroked her bared legs before removing her boots and socks and setting them aside.

A shiver raced from her throat and settled in her breasts at the warmth of Mark's hands compared to Sam's cool touch. Soon she'd have both hands touching her, fondling her, dominating her.

"Such pretty feet," he murmured as he fastened matching leather restraints around her ankles.

"What are you going to do with me?" Her voice was breathless as she ran through the various possible punishments the two men might have devised. Would they interrogate her using the good cop/bad cop technique? Would she get to go down on one while the other fucked her, just like she'd fantasized?

"Ah, sweet pea, I'm not gonna tell you—that would ruin the

anticipation now, wouldn't it? And just so you can't cheat and see what we've got planned..." Sam stuck his hand in his pocket, retrieving a blindfold.

He placed it over her eyes and tied it in place, extinguishing all light. "You see anything?"

"No."

"You wouldn't lie to me now, would you?"

She shook her head, slightly losing her balance in the process.

Mark grabbed one elbow, Sam the other, as they walked her out of the office and into the hall. They turned in the opposite direction she'd come and walked what felt like the length of the thickly carpeted hall before they stopped. There was a whirring noise and they walked her forward a few paces onto a tiled surface then stopped, turned her around. The floor lurched beneath her feet.

The elevator the previous owner had installed.

But was she going up or down? Up, she decided.

The motion stopped and she heard the door slide open. They led her out and to the left. Disoriented because of the blindfold, she tried to recall the floor plan she'd studied. The sounds changed when they turned her and she realized they'd taken her into a large room. Yes, they had to be in the master bedroom. She frowned when she heard the sound of a pocket door scraping in its tracks right in front of her and then was led forward. The thick carpet cushioning her bare feet changed to cool tile. They were taking her into the bathroom? Ah, yes, Sam liked the whirlpool.

She heard the scrape as another panel moved then a clicking sound, like a code being entered into a keypad. Wait a minute, there was no other room off the master bathroom.

"Watch your step, Jodi," Mark urged. "We're going downstairs."

Downstairs? There was nothing in the blueprints about stairs off the master bathroom—and why would they have taken her up in the first place? She slid her foot along the tile and tentatively felt in front of her until she found the step.

"And again." Then a third step, and a fourth. After fourteen they finally stopped on a concrete floor.

"Mark?" she whispered, suddenly unsure of her decision.

"It's all right, babe. Sam's had a safe room built—we're going to be using it tonight." Mark rubbed her arm as they lead her down what felt like a narrow corridor before she heard the metallic creak of a heavy door opening.

"Hit the light switch there, will you, Mark?" she heard Sam say.

Light glimmered from beneath the edges of the blindfold.

"This way, sweet pea." Sam took her arm and lead her a few more paces before saying, "Lift your foot and step up."

After taking the step, and being turned around, Jodi took a deep breath, forcing herself to relax. Bound and blindfolded, led to a room that didn't exist? So far, this definitely was not her idea of a fun evening.

After Mark released the clasp fastening her wrists together, he massaged her shoulders. "Relax, babe. Wait'll you see this place. We're going to have a blast."

"All set?" Sam said after a few moments.

Jodi swallowed then nodded. As one, they lifted her arms as high as her shoulders. She heard a metallic clinking, then their hands dropped away, leaving her arms suspended in mid-air. A fresh shiver of anticipation crawled up her spine and under the skin of her arms.

"Can you move?" Mark said from just in front of her.

She pulled on the restraints but her bonds didn't budge. Hopefully they wouldn't leave her here too long—the blood would drain out of her hands.

Something cold and hard—metallic—touched her right biceps. After a slight tug, it slid to her shoulder and along the seam to her neck. The fabric slithered down her front, baring one breast. She could feel her nipple puckering under the blast of air-conditioned air from a vent above her.

They were *cutting* her clothes off her? Thank God Mark had brought one of the company tees rather than something from her closet.

The sensation was repeated on her left arm. Soon her top slithered down her belly and came to rest on her bare feet.

"You have real pretty tits, sweet pea. You nipples are like ripe berries waiting to be plucked."

"She thinks they're too small," Mark said with a chuckle.

"And I'm sure Mark's told you that more than a mouthful's wasted."

Heat rose up her neck. Being naked was never a hang-up for her, but being naked in front of another man while Mark watched. Would he be jealous? Or did he not feel the way she would if he was viewing another woman? Maybe he didn't love her the way she loved him.

A tongue swept over her right nipple, but she couldn't tell whose. Warm breath moved across her cleavage, then lips laved her left breast, teeth nipping lightly. "Taste as sweet as berries too."

Fire swirled in her breast and shot straight to her pussy when she realized it was Sam touching her, kissing her. It shouldn't feel so good to know another man was arousing her when Mark was right there.

Should it?

The cool edge of the knife touched first one hip, then the other, and her pants slid over her ankles.

Two sets of lips kissed her almost reverently—one kissing her belly button, the other feathering down the small of her back.

“You’re beautiful, sweet pea,” Sam whispered from behind. “You should see how turned on Mark is right now. How much he wants you.”

Warm lips pressed against the back of her neck as a hand cupped her breast. “Isn’t she beautiful, Mark?”

“Oh yeah.” Mark’s voice sounded strained. “I’m so hard I ache, babe.”

“Now be a good little burglar and lift your foot,” Sam said from her left side.

She did and felt the remnants of her clothes being pulled from her ankle.

“Now your right foot,” Mark said from that side.

When she put her foot back down on the ground, two sets of hands wrapped gently around her ankles.

“Spread your legs, babe.”

They fastened the ankle restraints, leaving her standing spread-eagled, unable to move. A fly captured in a spider’s web.

Two sets of hands ran up her calves, her thighs. Fingers parted her cleft, dipped forward into moisture coating her labia, then traced back and circled the tight bud of her rear.

“I’ll bet your ass is so tight my dick’ll feel like it’s been taken to heaven when I’m fucking it, won’t it, sweet pea?” Sam whispered as his finger broached deeper, his breath a warm caress against her ass. A hiss of indrawn breath revealed

Mark's location.

The idea of someone else—of Sam—fucking her while Mark watched sent volatile fireballs to every nerve ending in both her pussy and her ass. How could she have considered leaving earlier?

"Punishment time, Jodi," Mark whispered in her ear. Her heart immediately raced as if she'd been running.

A marathon.

Up the side of a mountain.

The sharp whistling sound of...what was that? It reminded her of a whip, or a belt arcing through the air. Her butt tightened at the thought of being paddled or spanked as her punishment.

"Now, sweet pea, we're going to play a game. If you guess correctly, you get rewarded. If you guess incorrectly, you'll be punished."

"What do I have to do?"

Lips touched hers. Lips tasting of cigar smoke. "You have to guess which one of us—"

"—is doing what to you," Mark finished, nibbling just below her ear.

"Someone's gonna touch you..."

"When whatever they're doing stops you have to say who it was."

They were circling her, trying to confuse her.

"If you get it wrong..."—something whistled through the air, stung her ass in a thin line—"then you'll be punished."

Heat gathered in the cheek where she'd been hit. Mark had only ever used the flat of his hand, but the thin instrument they'd just used focused the sensation, which shot straight to her core. "And if I get it right?"

"Then, sweet pea, you'll be rewarded."

"How?"

"You'll find that out when that happens."

"But you have to get one right, first."

"And to make it a bit more of a challenge for you, your time will be limited." Someone's palm—Mark's she guessed—smacked flat against her ass again, blurring the thin line of heat from the last hit. "Hmm. She liked your riding crop better. You know, I think I might try out some of your toys."

"Be my guest, there's enough to choose from," Sam said with a chuckle.

Jodi wiggled her ass in anticipation.

"Oh, and, sweet pea? If you don't answer quick enough, you'll be punished no matter what your answer."

She heard the sound of something rattle, then snapped through the air. Was that a... It sounded like it had multiple tails. A flogger?

"Are you prepared to accept our punishment?" Mark asked.

"Yes." More than ready. Cream leaked down her thigh in a torturous tickle.

Seconds later, a hand caressed her left breast. Cool but gentle fingers tweaked her nipple. She rolled her head back, arching at the sensation when a tongue swirled across her other taut peak, teeth nipping lightly. The hint of cigar wafted up. A smile curled her lips—she would soon find out what her reward would be.

Too soon the touching, the licking, stopped. The sudden lack of contact left her panting, wanting more.

"Time to guess, Jodi," Mark said from her left side. "Was it me?"

"Or me," Sam whispered from her right side.

A wicked thought occurred to her; she struggled to stop her smile from showing. She enjoyed Mark punishing her, and the anticipation of discovering what rewards they had planned would be that much more intense. Besides she always did prefer being the bad girl to the good.

"Mark."

"Wrong!"

Even though she was expecting it she jumped when the flogger whistled and cracked with a thwack against her tender skin. The heat in her buttocks spread straight to her pussy.

"I'm not sure she thought that a punishment, ol' buddy," Sam said with a chuckle.

A large warm palm flattened over her belly, fingers spread wide, played with her belly button ring. They moved lower, parting her labia. Hot breath tickled her navel as someone kneeling in front of her exhaled. A finger—or was that a thumb?—rubbed beside the sensitive bundle of nerves that ached to be touched, slipped around it, below, never satisfying her need.

"Please," she whimpered. She squirmed, trying to force the digit over that spot.

The movement stopped, the traitorous hand withdrew She jumped when the crop stung her ass again.

"But I haven't guessed yet!"

"You moved. That's against the rules," Mark said from her right.

"You will stand still when we touch you, or we will leave you hanging there and not touch you again," Sam said from her left. "Now tell us who it was who made you so needy?"

She tried to guess who it might have been...

"Tick tock, sweet pea."

...there had been no scent of cigar, no creak of leather...

"Five, four, three—"

"Mark!"

Sam heaved a long sigh, and from the sound, she got the feeling he was shaking his head.

"It wasn't?" Wouldn't she have been spanked for guessing wrong?

"No, sweet pea, you were right, but I'm disappointed that you've not credited me yet." He let out another dramatic sigh.

"You still owe me a reward," she reminded him.

"You're right, we do."

After a moment, she sensed movement—someone knelt directly in front of her. Warm breath caressed her breast, a tongue swiped over one nipple then drew it into his mouth and began to suckle. One hand caressed her ass, another slipped between her legs. A finger slid inside. A second. Then a third, fucking her until every nerve ending inside her threatened to burst into flame. She nearly cried when they withdrew.

"Let's see what you can earn next," Mark said.

Calloused hands caressed her ass, broad fingers parted her cheeks. A tongue laved from front to back, rimming her.

"Sam."

Someone—Mark? or Sam?—sucked her nipples as a finger trailed through her cream, drew it back along her ass. It circled her tight bud then nudged inside, waiting as her muscles adjusted to the invasion. Her suspicion that it was Sam was confirmed when rough stubble abraded her inner thighs. Sam tongued the throbbing bundle of nerves, then thrust his tongue into her pussy. A second finger joined the first, stretching her ass wider, then both thrust in time with his tongue. Just as she was ready to leap over the edge, the fingers and mouths withdrew.

Shaking with her need, she cried, "No! Please! I need to come."

Fire licked in Mark's belly, tightened like a vise about his chest, as he watched Sam laving Jodi's clit with a tenderness he hadn't expected. Watched her arch her back, heard her unsteady breathing, the breathy moan she made in her pleasure.

What the fuck was going on that he'd resent the hell out of his friend for doing exactly what he'd asked him to do? Damn it, he'd been the one who'd approached Sam and yet now he wanted to pull him off Jodi, to ram his fist into Sam's face.

Sam's gaze flicked over to him, rested briefly on the flogger in his hand. Mark glanced down and realized he'd gripped it so hard his knuckles were white.

When Sam resumed tonguing her glistening pussy, Mark took a step back. Closed his eyes so he wouldn't see how she rotated her hips toward Sam's mouth. Tried to close his ears to the sound of Jodi's soft whimpers. Whimpers he wanted to be for him. Only him.

"Please," Jodi pleaded. "Please, Sam, please let me come. I really need this."

Mark's teeth ground so hard, he swore sparks would shoot from his mouth. She should be begging *him* to make her come, not Sam. What made him think Jodi was someone he could stand by and watch as someone else fucked her?

He opened his eyes to find Sam picking up the crop he'd set down.

"No moving, remember?" Sam gave Mark a curious look as he snapped the crop across Jodi's ass.

Her thighs quivered as if they tried to close, to press together and ease the ache he heard in her voice.

God, she was so beautiful. So responsive.

Beneath her blindfold, he knew her eyelids would be heavy from sexual arousal. His hand lifted of its own accord, hovered over Jodi's full bottom lip, wanting to stroke it; his body leaned in until he could feel the heat of her body brush his. He wanted to drop to his knees and kiss the taut, budded nipples, hear her beg for more attention. His attention.

He'd go down on her, taste that wonderful cream streaming down her thighs. Suck on her clit, use his fingers against that spot that he knew drove her insane. He'd bring her to orgasm again and again, and each time she'd scream his name. *His* name. No one else's. Ever.

But after he'd gone to Sam and suggested this evening, after he'd convinced Jodi it would be fun, how could he back out? How could he tell Sam to leave? He'd look like a first-class idiot.

"Such a pretty pink ass you've got, sweet pea," Sam said. "And your pussy is so wet it's dripping down your thighs like Niagara Falls. Hey, Mark, hand me that cloth, will you, buddy?"

When Sam's large hand caressed her ass and Jodi moaned her approval, Mark's vision went red.

Chapter Six

"Here you go." A dark anger reverberated through Mark's voice, a threatening tone she'd heard only once before—when a suspect had attacked her from behind. She wished she could see his face, see into his eyes and know what he was thinking.

The sound of a scuffle and Mark's explosive "What the fuck!" had her tugging at her restraints but they held fast. Her vulnerability slapped her harder than any flogging she'd had that night, squeezed the breath from her lungs.

Footsteps—shuffling noises, grunts—came from behind her.

"What the fuck are you doing, Watson? Get off me!"

There was a bang as if someone had been shoved into a wall and a rattling noise as something skittered across the floor.

"Mark! Mark?" Her breath came in short, quick gasps while her legs could barely support her. "Mark, what's happening? What's the matter? Sam, what are you doing? Let him go!"

"I'm doing this for your own good, buddy."

"You hurt Jodi, I'll fucking kill you, Watson." The undercurrent of fear in Mark's voice sent ice cubes tumbling down Jodi's spine. "I'll cut off your balls and shove 'em so far down your throat they'll come out your ass."

Flesh smacked on flesh and Sam grunted. "Goddamn it,

buddy, you're wrigglier than a greased pig. I've just changed up the plan, that's all."

Sam's voice came closer. She pulled back as far as the restraints allowed her, which meant she could barely move.

"Now don't you fuss there, sweet pea, if that boyfriend of yours would just shut his face for a minute, I think you'll both agree to my little change of plan."

Jodi blinked in the light as Sam gently peeled the blindfold from her face.

"It's all right, honey, I'm not going to hurt you. But you'd better slow down your breathin' before you pass out." He cupped her face with his huge hand. "In through your nose and out through your mouth, all right?"

Somewhat dazed that she was trusting him, she followed his direction, forcing air into steel-banded lungs. The trembling in her legs and arms gradually subsided.

"That's it, sweet pea. Remember, I would never do anything you didn't want me to do. I'm going to let you free, but first you have to promise to listen to my proposal, all right?"

"Mark?" she asked, forcing air from her lungs. "What have you done with Mark?"

After a moment's hesitation, Sam moved aside.

Her eyes widened to see Mark lying on a gargantuan bed. Heavy leather straps restrained his arms and legs, spread-eagled until he resembled a prisoner in the dungeon of a medieval castle. Except the bright room she found herself in resembled no medieval castle she'd ever seen.

Mirrors lining the walls and ceiling reflected the bed. Overstuffed multicolored pillows of various shapes were scattered across the floor, dislodged from the bed no doubt by Mark's struggles. A giant flat-screen television loomed at the end of the bed, a second hung over the headboard, yet another was mounted flat within the mirrored ceiling for the ultimate viewing experience from any angle. A leather sling hung in one corner while chairs and a bench had been grouped by a large unlit fireplace. More cushions and wedges covered in leather and velvet and silk were heaped upon them but didn't hide the leather restraints on the arms.

There was no ambiguity about the purpose of the room—it had been designed for every sexual position that she could have dreamed of—and several she couldn't.

Mark glared at their captor as he continued cursing Sam, a look so fierce on his face that Jodi shivered. She'd seen Mark in action, seen how he could take down an armed opponent barehanded. To be chained, pinned, useless would be torture for him. And yet there was something so provocative, so compelling about having Mark bound. Would Sam let her have a say in what directions their games would now take?

"Trust me, Jodi. Please," Sam said quietly. "I'm just changing the original plans Mark and I worked out, that's all. But I think you'll both enjoy what I've got planned."

Mark's scowl darkened. "Just what has that perverted mind of yours dreamed up this time, Watson?"

Sam smiled at Jodi, though a cautious look shadowed his eyes. "He calls *me* perverted after he suggested tonight's entertainment."

His light-hearted gibe belied the worry lines crinkling his forehead, and the way he kept glancing between her and Mark. He obviously wasn't as sure they'd approve of his plan as his tone implied.

"Will you promise that when I let you go, you won't attack me? Will you at least hear me out?"

She caught her bottom lip between her teeth, wondering

how to interpret the dark look Mark shot her. He'd arranged the game, he'd trusted Sam. Now it was up to her to trust Mark's judgment.

A slight nod of her head gave him her answer.

"Thank you." Sam knelt beside her and began to unfasten the leather strap attaching her ankle to one of the two posts she'd been tied to. Despite her assurance she'd listen to him, he kept the post between them so she couldn't easily kick him. But then why should he trust her given how he'd betrayed Mark's trust?

After Sam freed both Jodi's ankles, he flipped open the clasp restraining her right arm, took her wrist in his and chafed it between his palms. He freed her left hand, and massaged that wrist too. She glanced down and saw just how huge his hands were as they engulfed her small one, felt the power in them and knew they could snap her bones as easy as a dry twig. Yet he held her so gently she might have been a baby bird cradled in his palms.

"You go check for yourself that your boyfriend's all right but don't undo those restraints until I tell you. Will you promise me that?"

"All right," she agreed finally.

"Good girl." He patted her behind. "Climb up on the bed and rest your pretty ass. I'll explain more in a second."

She walked across the room, the mirrors reflecting every angle of her body. Being naked had never been a big concern for her, but there was definitely something erotic to being so exposed considering both men were still fully dressed.

"You okay, babe?" Mark asked quietly, calmer now she was free and sitting beside him, though his fierce frown toward Sam did not abate.

As she assured him she was, she looked back at the dais. She gasped at what had been behind her. Whips, floggers and paddles had been arranged in ornate patterns on the wall behind the two posts. Cock rings, nipple clamps, ball gags, hoods and masks filled the glass-fronted cabinets on each side.

"Sam's got some...unusual tastes. That's why I thought of him when I was planning this." Mark jerked at the chains trapping him in place. "I *thought* I could trust him when I suggested it."

Sam chuckled. "Still can, ol' buddy, still can."

"Mark," she whispered. "Do you want me to let you go?"

He scrunched his eyes closed and exhaled. "You made the list—do you want to continue?"

Sam's change of plans concerned her. But having Mark at her mercy, especially after the game they'd just played with her, was intriguing. "Can we trust him?"

He frowned as Sam walked over to a cabinet and opened a door, revealing a laptop computer. There was something at the back of his eyes, like he was waging a war within himself. His hands curled into fists, his shoulder muscles tightened and a muscle in his jaw twitched before he said, "Yeah, we can trust him."

But she thought he heard him mutter *I think* under his breath.

Well, great. He obviously wasn't comfortable with the change in plans despite his assurances.

"Now, I'll bet you're both wondering why I changed things up." Sam ignored Mark's growl. "You know we were roommates in college, right?"

Jodi nodded.

"Did he tell you how he used to watch me fucking my

dates?"

She shook her head. From the corner of her eye, she saw Mark grimacing as he turned his head away from Sam. While she knew Mark loved to watch her play with herself with her vibrator, strangely the idea of Mark watching other women being fucked irritated her. So much for their little agreement not to become possessive with each other. Obviously Mark hadn't the same problem, considering he was voluntarily sharing her with Sam.

His smile fading, Sam drummed his fingers on his thigh as if he were rethinking whatever he'd had planned.

"So he'd watch you with your dates..." she prompted.

After a moment, he continued, "We worked out a system where I'd pretend to sneak them into the room, telling them he was asleep—they'd get off on the idea of having to be so quiet and not wake him up. Liked the danger of getting caught, I guess."

"But he'd really be awake the whole time, watching?"

"Sometimes he did more than just watch, sweet pea. Sometimes he'd join in. And then there were the times we reversed the game, and he brought his girlfriends for us to share." Sam lifted a ball gag from its hook, hefted it in his hand as he eyed Mark. "I'm thinkin' you deserve to be punished for not telling your girlfriend all this yourself."

Mark narrowed his eyes, a fierce scowl on his face. "Try it and you'll find that ball the only one you have left to play with tomorrow."

"No? No." Sam lobbed the ball gag back onto the table. "Anyway, to get to the point—"

"Too late," Mark grumbled.

"Point is," Sam continued as if he hadn't heard Mark's gibe, “since Mark didn’t give you a choice about who joined you in the threesome, I reckoned that you might enjoy helping me torture your boyfriend a little. Give him a real show of the two of us enjoyin’ ourselves. You know, a little turnabout being fair play and all. So are you up for my little change in plans, sweet pea?”

Chapter Seven

Something about Sam's explanation didn't quite ring true. While she didn't doubt the games they'd played in college, after all she already knew of Mark's voyeuristic tendencies, a molten undercurrent rippled between the two men. Not a macho my-dick-is-bigger-than-yours type game, but a quicksilver explosiveness from Mark, and though Sam tried to conceal it, an underlying wariness that she hadn't sensed from him at the beginning of the night.

During the game, they'd worked together with no animosity. So why had Sam felt it necessary to change the rules partway through? And was it Sam's change that had Mark glowering? Or was he simply angry at the control Sam had taken by force?

Mark definitely didn't like relinquishing control. After she'd suggested the little bondage game they'd enjoyed the week before, she'd expected that he would return the favor, let her tie him up and explore what it was like to be so completely in charge. But to her disappointment, and annoyance, he'd refused.

Is that was this was about? A "King of the Monkey bars" game between the two friends?

Men, she huffed. Fine, if he wanted to play that type of game, she'd play right along. Wouldn't hurt to take some control back from Mark after he'd manipulated this whole evening. Since he liked watching, she'd give him a show he'd never forget. With Sam's assistance, of course. She wondered if Sam could wrestle Mark up onto the dais so she could use the flogger on his ass.

When she didn't answer, Sam glanced over at her and smiled as he pocketed something. He walked toward them in an almost-predatory stalk.

"Hey, Mark, I think she likes the idea. Look at her tight little nipples, at how wide her pupils are. She's so turned on she can't even answer." He tapped Jodi on the shoulder, interrupting her fantasies. "So what's it going to be, sweet pea? We gonna have some more fun? Or are you gonna wimp out and call it a night? It's your decision."

His quiet question allowed the last of her concerns about Sam to float away like a feather in a breeze. He had no intention of harming her or keeping her captive. Just as Mark had originally assured her.

"Nothing's changed on my side. Mark promised me a night I'd never forget." She smiled at Mark. "And since Sam's delivered you up on a silver platter, looks like now we'll both have a memorable evening."

Jodi walked two fingers up Mark's leg, slid between his thighs and cupped his groin. When his hips jerked and his breath hissed through clenched teeth, her lips curved into a smile. "What's the matter, big guy? You enjoyed torturing me earlier with your little game. Can't handle a little return attention?"

He stared at her from beneath lowered lids, a muscle in his jaw ticking. "I can take whatever you dish out, babe."

"We'll see if you feel the same after the games I plan to play."

"You've got quite a woman here, Mark."

Another frisson of dark energy snaked between the two men before Mark shrugged in a stiff gesture. "Just so long as you back off if she tells you."

"That's a given, ol' buddy. Sweet pea, you remember your safe word? It still applies, all right?" One thick brow beetled up, waiting for her answer.

Whatever aggression was bleeding from Mark, at least it wasn't directed at her. As well it shouldn't be considering he'd been tonight's architect.

"The safe word is still broccoli." She arched a cool look at Mark.

"Will you let me try a few things I noticed weren't on your list?" Sam asked.

The sight of the big man patiently waiting on her answer sent a thrill up her spine. She'd be in control of not only Mark but of him too. Except what had she forgotten to put on her list? "Yes, I trust you."

Sam rolled her nipples between his thumb and forefinger then reached into his pocket and pulled out an earring. No. Not an earring, she realized as he opened one end and clamped it over her nipple. He tugged gently, causing her pussy to clamp down and weep at the pleasure/pain it created. A moan escaped her when he attached the second clamp and tugged on them both.

Wow, nipple clamps weren't something she'd considered—they'd always looked painful. How could she have known she'd be brought nearly to orgasm by them?

"Hurt too bad?"

"No," she stammered. "It just feels..." How could pain feel so good? She must be a freak to enjoy it so much.

Seeming to understand her confusion, Sam held out his hands. "Give me your hands, sweet pea."

After a moment's hesitation, Jodi placed her hands in his only to find herself dragged facedown crosswise over Mark's lap once more. Sam moved away, out of her line of sight. She heard more tapping into the computer, then he walked to the other side of the bed and gently stroked her pussy.

"She's so responsive, isn't she, Mark?" Sam said quietly. "You see how her hips are moving as I touch her?"

Mark's cock stirred beneath her belly, pressing into her as it thickened. Sam had been right—Mark would get off watching them fuck.

Sam made a show of licking her juices from his fingers. "Why she's as sweet as a Georgia peach."

"Enjoy it while you can, Watson," Mark sneered. "You'll never get another chance to taste her again."

A smoldering possessiveness matching the warning in his voice made her turn her head to stare at Mark. Something dark flashed in his eyes—was he jealous? Angry? Or just incredibly turned on?

Sam patted her cheeks and walked around the bed to the other side of the room. "Stick your beautiful ass up in the air as high as you can, sweet pea. We want to make sure Mark has a good view, after all."

She adjusted her body as he'd directed, feeling a curious mix of vulnerability and excitement.

Sam typed something into the computer and grunted to himself. He scrolled the mouse and clicked a few times, then picked up a remote, aimed it at the televisions at each end of the bed.

Mark whistled softly as a picture of her ass filled the

monstrous screen. "Fuck, Sam, you got this room wired up that quickly?"

Sam grinned. "Hey, it's the twenty-first century, ol' buddy. Wide-screen, high-def plasma. Only the best for this boy. I'm recordin' it too—I'll give you the disk when we're done."

"What? Recording what?" Jodi scrambled upright, covering her breasts, only to realize the camera was now focusing on her crotch. With a foul curse, she grabbed the biggest pillow from the bed and held it in front of her. "No. No, this is not happening. I refuse to find this uploaded on YouTube tomorrow."

"Relax, sweet pea, you and Mark will have the only copy. I promise." Sam opened a cupboard beside the bed, pulled out a bag. He winked at her. "Of course if you choose to post it on the Net, I can't stop you. It won't hurt my reputation none."

Jodi shook her head. "No. No recording whatsoever. I don't like the idea of it falling into the wrong hands."

Sam's bottom lip jutted out, reminding Jodi of a child whose favorite toy had just been taken away.

Mark shared a look with Jodi, his gaze hot as he glanced at her barely covered breasts. "Can you leave the cameras on but not record?"

A smile slowly spread across Sam's face, lighting it up. "Sure can. Sweet pea, why don't you get back into position over Mark's lap?"

As she repositioned herself, she heard him tapping on the laptop and suddenly different images appeared on the screens. The one over the bed zoomed in on Mark's face, the one at the end of the bed showed an up-close-and-personal view of her glistening labia.

She squirmed as the camera zoomed out slightly, and her ass came into view. As if she didn't feel self-conscious enough about her butt; seeing it in high-definition wide-screen wasn't exactly good for the ego. Instead she concentrated on Mark, on the sweat gathering on his forehead. He wasn't watching the television at all, but her ass. She wiggled her hips to deliberately taunt him. A bead of sweat rolled down his temple, his hands flexing on the chains as if he wanted to reach out and touch her.

Sam opened a cabinet beside the bed and removed a box, placing it on the coverlet beside her. "I understand you enjoy a little anal play, Jodi. Or was Mark shinin' me on?"

Jodi turned her head to stare at the bulge in Sam's pants. The muscles in her ass clenched at the thought of being penetrated by the thick cock outlined in black leather. "Um, I like it when *he* does it."

A grin split Sam's face when he saw where Jodi was looking. He cupped his bulging groin. "You worrying that ol' Sam Junior here's not gonna fit into that tight little ass of yours? Well now, you don't worry 'bout a thing, sweet pea, 'cause I'm gonna prepare you so it won't hurt."

"Go slow, Sam, she's real tight," Mark warned, which made her ass tighten even more.

Moments later, she felt the bed dip beneath Sam's weight. Huge gel-covered fingers came into the camera's view, briefly hovered over her ass. They separated her cheeks, spread the cool gel around her entrance. One finger penetrated her knuckle-deep, pressed farther, spreading the gel deep inside of her. Watching what Sam was doing on the wide screen, and feeling it at the same time was a strange sensation but knowing Mark was watching another man touching her ass was a turn-on she'd never expected.

Her eyes widened when a bright red butt plug came into view, pressed against her opening. That sucker was huge, way bigger than any man's cock she'd ever seen. And definitely bigger than the plug Mark had bought for her when they'd first tried anal sex.

"It's too big." Her breath caught in her throat. She tried to move away but his hands held her firmly in place.

"It's just the camera—remember they say it adds ten pounds?" Sam chuckled.

He leaned over, his leather pants cool against the back of her thighs as he whispered into her ear, "Trust me. I know how much Mark loves watching me fucking a woman's ass."

Mark groaned. "Way to remind Jodi of my past lovers, Watson."

Sam caressed her neck, then moved lower, easing the tension that had crept into her shoulders. But for all his efforts, Jodi tensed when the tip of the plug intruded.

"Just take nice slow, deep breaths, and think how much fun it's going to be tormenting old Mark over there."

"You don't have to do this, Jodi," Mark rasped. "You can still tell him to stop."

"I'm okay." Her ass burning, she scrunched her eyes closed as the plug penetrated the first tight ring.

"Just relax, Jodi. Remember to breathe." Sam pressed the plug deeper in a relentless motion. "I'm not hurting you now, am I, sweet pea?"

Jodi shook her head. "No, it just feels weird knowing it's not Mark touching me there."

And hot. So hot. Her pussy ached to be filled too.

"Open your eyes. Watch how hot Mark's getting. See how he's straining against those restraints?"

Mark's lips were white as he captured them between his teeth, the veins in his biceps stood out in stark relief as his grip on the chains tightened.

Sam whispered, his free hand stroking her ass in a gentle caress. "He's like a dog ready to attack. To protect you. Or to take you for his own."

With a smooth movement, Sam pushed the butt plug up as far as it would go, then pulled her from Mark's lap until she was draped over his arm like a femme fatale in a thirties movie. A sizzling jolt shot up her spine when he tugged on the nipple clamp with his teeth. With a final tug, he lay her down beside Mark and returned to the laptop.

"Spread your legs real wide for me. You can lean against Mark if you want but face out so I can taste your sweet honey some more."

Squirming until she was cradled between Mark's arm and body, she arranged her legs at the side of bed and rested her head on Mark's chest. Despite the size of the plug that stretched her ass, she was surprisingly comfortable. Though it was definitely larger than the one she had at home, this plug really wasn't as big as it had looked. It must have been the camera accentuating the size, she decided.

The images on the television changed to two of her from different angles, one zoomed in close to her groin, the other showing her full body from above the bed. Sam crawled onto the bed and lifted one of her legs over his shoulder. With a bright grin, he glanced up at her. "I've been looking forward to this all night."

He lowered his head. Fascinated, Jodi watched on the big screen as he ran his tongue up her labia, felt the thick warmth swirl in intricate patterns, never quite touching her clitoris. The carnal intrusion shot bolts of energy to every nerve ending, starting a smoldering fire that quickly burst into a conflagration when his tongue finally touched her core.

She grabbed at the silk comforter on either side of her hips, gasping, arching her hips. A broad hand lay flat across her belly, holding her in place.

"Don't make me tie you down too." His words rippled against her sensitized flesh, rumbled through her bones and set off another firestorm.

"Jodi? Open your eyes. Look at Mark."

When had she closed them? Her lids heavy, she turned her head and saw sweat running down Mark's brow, his fingers alternately opening then closing around the chains.

"Oh, baby, I wish that was me going down on you." His voice sounded rough, like he'd been singed by the flames she was sure were shooting from her.

Sam drew back for a moment and dragged a finger over her labia, dipped it into her pussy. He smeared her cream across her mouth then dipped his head again, thrusting his tongue into her pussy.

"Let me lick it off you, baby," Mark whispered. "Let me taste what Sam's tasting."

Arching her back, Jodi captured Mark's mouth with her own, tasting the salty sweat on his upper lip. He thrust his tongue into her mouth, mimicking Sam's motions.

In desperation, her hands sought Mark's erection. Sam grabbed her hands and pushed them firmly by her side.

"Oh, no, none of that. He just gets to watch this time."

Sam resumed his attentions, one hand tugging on a nipple clamp, sending a bolt of heat straight to her pussy, and her blood boiling through her veins. He slipped one finger inside her, then another. When he pressed on the butt plug while this tongue flicked just the right place, she shattered.

With an easy movement, Sam tugged his shirt off. Her eyes

widened to see a long, ugly scar marring his chest, but then he undid his fly, letting his leathers fall to the floor. His scar forgotten, Jodi sucked in a breath at the sight of his cock, and knew he hadn't misjudged the need for such a big butt plug.

He hopped onto the bed and arranged the pillows beside Mark, ensuring he didn't come close to Mark's hand, and lay down.

"Crawl on up here, sweet pea. Let me feel that soft mouth of yours on Sam Junior."

She stifled her snort. There was nothing *junior* about that thick pole. While his cock was the same length as Mark's, it was thicker. He slid his hand along its length and back down, squeezing the tip on each pass, a bead of pearly moisture glistening at its tip.

"Don't take your eyes off Mark." As she caught Mark's gaze, she saw the hunger deep in his eyes. The lust. And something deeper, almost feral.

"Start off licking my balls," Sam commanded. His hand lifted them as his hips thrust closer to her.

With each swipe of her tongue, Mark's breathing got heavier, his eyes half closing.

"Now lick my cock, sweet pea. Make a meal of me."

She began with a teasing nip to the base of his shaft, then swirled her tongue up the thick shaft, tracing the dark veins that bulged from the taut skin. Her eyes still on Mark, she made a show of spreading the drop of come that quivered at the end of *Junior's* slit over her lips. Then delicately, slowly, licked it off.

Feeling power spread through her at having such a captive audience, Jodi opened her mouth, tightened her lips over Junior's head and swallowed him deep.

"Watch her, Mark. Look at how her lips are stretching over my shaft. Oh shit, that feels so good!" Sam threw his head back and arched his hips as she increased the suction. The noise of her sucking and Mark's harsh pants mingled with Sam's murmured instructions.

Jodi tasted a trickle of pre-come on the back of her tongue, slightly more acidic than Mark's essence. Her hand drifted down between her legs, thrust inside in a feeble attempt to mimic the motions of her mouth, her tongue. Cream coated her fingers, slid down her thighs as her hips thrust. She rolled her clit between her thumb and forefinger, moaning as the pressure inside her built like a volcano about to explode.

Fingers wrapped in her hair forcing her to resume the movement she'd forgotten while pleasuring herself. Eventually he held her head still, his hips pistoning his cock deep into her mouth.

"She's giving me the best blow job I've ever had, Mark. But you know that, don't you? I'll bet you're wishing...her lips were...around your cock, aren't you?" Sam said, his voice deepening with every thrust. "Isn't her ass beautiful? Can you imagine me...parting those sweet cheeks of hers...taking her ass?"

Chapter Eight

Sam's taunts caused Mark's guts to cramp like he'd swallowed a length of razor wire.

What had he been thinking, suggesting a threesome with Sam? Why had he thought he'd be okay sharing Jodi with any man, let alone a player like Sam?

Jodi moaned, her hand moving frantically between her arching hips as Sam thrust his dick down her throat. Mark wanted to plant a fist in Sam's face when he saw his friend's eyes scrunched closed, a look of ecstasy on his face. Ecstasy from Jodi sucking him off. They'd discussed a similar scenario, but he was supposed to be satisfying Jodi from behind while she went down on Sam. And he'd never thought about what it would feel like, how his heart would tear watching Sam enjoying Jodi's attentions. It had never mattered before with any of their girlfriends in college.

Why had Sam changed up their plan? Despite what Sam had told Jodi, he knew his friend had some hidden reason for tying him to the bed and forcing him to watch the two of them fucking. But what?

Jodi's cheeks hollowed and her neck worked as she swallowed. Sam's groan made Mark's cock ache as it remembered what it felt like to be deep-throated by Jodi. Remembered how it felt to have that wonderful tongue of hers caress every millimeter of sensitive skin. Remembered the amazing suction she had, coaxing every last drop of come from his balls.

He shifted his hips, attempting to relieve the pain in his cock, not only from being trapped beneath too-tight denim, but from its need to bury itself in her, to feel those tight muscles grasp him, contract around him as she found her release. Yet here he was—a spectator.

For what felt like the fiftieth time that night, Mark grasped the chains binding him to the bed and tugged in a futile effort to free himself. He had to stop this travesty. He had to snatch Jodi away from Sam and finish within her. Hear her scream her release. A release only he could bring her.

Then he'd take Sam down—crush his balls, cut off his dick—whatever it took to punish him for daring to take Jodi in front of him like this. And yell at Jodi for agreeing to Sam's suggestion.

His head fell back on the pillow, his conscience mocking him with a taunting laugh. Hell, who was he kidding? He'd been the one who had suggested, no, forced Jodi to write that damned list of fantasies. He'd been the one who had initially suggested the whole idea to Sam, not the other way around. He'd been the one to talk Jodi into the whole idea upstairs. And now he was the one trapped in a nightmare caused by his own hubris. Forced to watch his lover bringing his best friend to the height of ecstasy.

Another deep-throated moan escaped Jodi's lips. Mark closed his eyes as his cock pulsed, remembering the feel of those moans the last time she'd gone down on him. His spine tingled and his hips arched, seeking relief. Seeking Jodi.

If he could just get free...

"Sam, at least release one hand so I can jerk off. This is

fucking torture to watch."

Without changing the rhythm of his hips, Sam opened his eyes. Shot a dark look of warning as he shook his head.

Goddamn it, what was that bastard playing at? It was like Sam expected him to know something. Understand something. But what?

Then all of a sudden Sam pulled his cock from Jodi's mouth. "Not yet."

A camera whirred overhead, the image on the screens capturing the moisture on Sam's still-erect cock. Caught a thin stream of come leaking from the slit and trickling down the head onto Jodi's mouth. Another camera zoomed in on Jodi's beautiful pink tongue as it skimmed over her bottom lip, and lingered on a glistening drop of Sam's come.

The barbed wire in his guts heated, snaked around his balls and tightened.

It should be his come she tasted. *His.*

What had possessed him to think he could sit idly by watching Jodi get off with another man, that he could share her? No man was ever going to touch her again. Only him. Jodi was his and his alone. And he was hers. Forever.

Whoa, where had that come from?

How many times had he and Sam shared their girlfriends back in college? Yet never before had he felt the icy-hot poker of jealousy now stabbing his gut. What was it about Jodi that caused him to feel like a guard dog protecting his property? His private property.

You're trying to pretend she's like all those other women you and Sam shared, his conscience mocked. *But she's not. You've fallen in love with her.*

"On your hands and knees, sweet pea."

If he'd been standing, he would have had to sit down and put his head between his knees. Holy shit, he loved her. Head-over-heels, deep-down-in-the-gut, 'til-death-do-us-part in love with her.

And stupid ass that he was, he'd voluntarily shared her with another man. He'd even encouraged her, told her it was okay to fuck someone else. And she'd agreed.

What if that meant... He swallowed hard, the barbed wire tightening until his balls felt like they were about to drop off. What if she didn't love him? What if when this was over, she wanted to have more threesomes, to force him to watch her fuck other men? Or worse, what if she stopped inviting him to join in?

Shit! What had he done?

A cold worm crawled through his intestines. A worm wearing razor-sharp spikes that ripped his guts apart as he remembered their agreement. After the first time they'd made love, he'd insisted there be no long-term attachments. That either one of them could walk away any time. And she'd agreed. Except, when he should have been clearing the mountains of paperwork he faced every day, he'd found himself fantasizing about fucking her on the desk, on the floor, against the wall. No, he amended, not fucking her, loving her.

"See okay there, buddy?"

Pulled from considering the ramifications of this revelation, Mark glanced over at Sam. Who smirked.

Is that what this was about? Did Sam realize that he loved Jodi before even he did? Was he trying to force Mark to get jealous? To acknowledge that Jodi was his and his alone? Knowing Sam, he'd never live that down.

"Ol' buddy?" Sam asked again, tilting his head toward the big screens. "You see okay?"

There in living Technicolor, larger than life, Jodi's ass filled the screen. The bright red butt plug a perfect target for Sam's goddamned cock.

His already-erect cock jerked as if trying to punch through the fly. Say no! it screamed. Stop this.

Sweat dripped down Mark's temples and his arms shook as they strained against the restraints. His mouth opened, wanting to tell them to stop. But the words stuck in his throat, tangled in the wire that ensnared his whole body.

What if she doesn't love me? How pathetic would that be?

Jodi stared at the flat-screen image as Sam's condom-covered cock bobbed into view. Watched it slide across her glistening swollen folds, watched as it buried itself into the dark pink opening stretching her drum-tight. Between the pressure of the plug up her ass and him stretching her pussy, she could feel every beat of his heart in the head of his cock.

A slow exhalation was followed by a moan as he began the gentle push and pull, exciting every inch of her, inside and out. "It's like a fucking velvet glove's wrapped around my dick."

Sam's fingers tightened on her hips as he began to rock into her, his movement quickly changing to a pounding rhythm. He reached around her front, one hand giving a nipple clamp a wicked tug, a movement that streaked to her core. The nipple clamps brushed the bulge in Mark's jean with each thrust of Sam's hips. Mark's hips pumped as if he were fucking her too.

Imagining freeing his cock, sucking it while Sam plowed into her drove her up to the edge of the abyss and pushed her over. Her hips bucked as her orgasm ripped through her in a wildfire of sensation.

"Not—done—yet." Sam groaned.

He slammed into her, burying himself to his balls, each time his stomach pressed against the butt plug, moving it just enough to drive her wild. If it was possible his cock thickened and pushed even deeper, stretching her until she thought she would burst.

When he stiffened and shouted, his hot stream of come pulsing hard inside her set off yet another firestorm. She shuddered through her orgasm, unable to gather breath enough to moan.

Sam caught her just before she collapsed onto Mark's lap, eased his cock from her body. "Damn, woman, I didn't want to come that soon."

"Come on, Sam. Let me free. I've got the mother of all hard-ons—my dick's hurtin' real bad here." Mark spoke through gritted teeth. Jodi opened her eyes and saw flames in the back of Mark's eyes, flames of lust, flames of fury.

A trickle of fear grew in her belly, tightening her diaphragm and driving the breath from her.

Had she made a mistake agreeing to Sam's plan? Mark was the one who had arranged this. *Hadn't that been what he'd wanted all along?* Shit, had she blown their relationship? Did he see her now only as a whore? Or was that what he thought of her in the first place to suggest this whole scenario? Could she convince him she wanted him more than anyone else?

Sam gestured with his head toward Mark. "All right, sweet pea, unzip loverboy's jeans. But that's all you're to do."

Seeing heat flash in Mark's eyes, she fumbled with his zipper. Yeah, she'd blown it. And the man she loved now despised her.

"Undo the restraints, Jodi," Mark ordered quietly so Sam couldn't hear.

If she let him go now, would he walk away? Not only from

the bed and the room but from her?

She licked her top lip when she saw his engorged cock outlined by the dark denim. A glance over her shoulder showed a bare-assed Sam fiddling with his computer, not paying any attention to what she was doing.

Her hands snaked around Mark's hips, and drew his jeans down to his knees. His underwear quickly followed suit. She shoved her hands under his ass and grabbed his buttocks while she licked the taut, satiny head. In a violent motion his hips arched up, shoved his cock through her lips until it touched her throat. God, he tasted so good! This felt so right. Wildly desperate, her nails dug into his ass, her mouth sucking, needing to make him come deep in her throat, needing to taste him.

The mattress dipped behind her. Fingers parted her labia and started playing with her clit. They moved expertly, pressing against her most sensitive areas, driving her wild with need. When two fingers penetrated her and stroked deep inside, she struggled to match the rhythm she knew Mark loved, needed.

Please don't pull me away, she silently pleaded to Sam.

Except Sam didn't hear her silent entreaty. Instead he withdrew his fingers and grasped her hips. Stopped her motion. Mark cursed volubly when Sam pulled her away.

"No," she moaned. "Please, Sam, I want to do this for Mark. I need him."

Sam leaned over her shoulder and whispered in her ear. "Then ride him, sweet pea."

Before Sam could retract his suggestion, Jodi swung her leg over Mark and sheathed him in one movement. She braced herself on his shoulders and rotated her hips, grinding his cock deep against her womb. All memory of Sam lost, she merged herself with Mark, their bodies moving in a sinuous dance. Just as she was climbing the final peak, she felt a hand on her shoulder, pressing her toward Mark.

“Let him suck those luscious tits,” Sam instructed.

“How am I supposed to suck them with these on?” Mark snagged one leather tassel in his teeth and growled. The pressure from the clamp pulled on her nipple, sending a bolt of lightning into her core.

Chuckling, Sam removed the nipple clamps and dropped them on the bed beside her. Mark laved the tender peaks. The soothing gesture was at odds to the fierce expression in his eyes; the soft words he murmured defied the bunched muscles in his arms and shoulders that threatened violence.

Sam said something but her mind was in such a whirl from Mark’s attentions that she didn’t hear. This—this was what she wanted. The two of them so close together she’d lost track of where she stopped and he began.

She was pulled from the brink when Sam pulled the butt plug out in a smooth movement.

His broad hand pressed against the back of her neck, laying her flat over Mark. “Don’t worry, sweet pea, you can keep lovin’ your man there. I’m just fixin’ to perform item number seven on your list.”

Her mind whirled, her thoughts a morass. What was item seven?

Oh shit! She’d said she wanted to have two men inside her at the same time. Did she want that? Should she tell him no? She buried her head in the crook of Mark’s neck. What would it be like to feel another cock warming her, caressing her in both places at the same time? Of course she wanted to try this. Look how empty she’d felt when he’d removed the butt plug. And she might never get another chance. She consciously relaxed against Mark and murmured, “All right.”

Thick fingers smeared cool gel over her ass and she felt that broad head nudge her tender opening. In a smooth movement, he pushed the head of his cock past the tight ring of her anus.

"Shit, Mark, she's so fuckin' tight." Sam groaned as he thrust into her deeper.

In an unconscious protest, she whimpered as Sam continued his relentless assault.

"Sam, stop, you're hurting her." Mark wrapped his hands on the chains holding him in place and pulled them tight. "Goddamn it, stop!"

"No, don't stop. Please," Jodi gasped. "Mark, he's not hurting me."

Sam curled over her, his wiry chest hair tickling her back. "Just relax, sweet pea, breathe."

Her whimper changed to a deep-throated moan as the hot pain of her ass combined with the white flare of pleasure in her pussy. Arching her back, she pushed against his shaft. Mark shifted inside her, the pressure of being stretched by the two cocks an erotic assault that sent fireballs rocketing through her system.

"Oh yeah, that's what I'm talkin' about." The slow glide stopped as he seated himself deep inside. He tenderly stroked her back as he waited for her to adjust.

He rocked into her in languid thrusts, pushing and pulling her cheeks apart as his cock stroked the walls of her ass.

Mark tilted his hips and began to match his movements to Sam's, never taking his gaze from Jodi's face.

"*Eres mia.*" Mark's eyes flashed and though whatever he'd said sounded beautiful, it wasn't said with his usual fluid grace. If anything, he ground out the words as a statement, a declaration. A challenge.

"*Eres mia, solo mia,*" he said again as he thrust deep within her.

"Do you know what he's saying?" Sam asked quietly.

Jodi shook her head.

He leaned closer, whispering so only she could hear. "He's saying '*you're mine, only mine.*'"

Tears filled her eyes at the translation. Did she dare hope that he loved her too?

"I'm yours, only yours," she whispered, pressing her lips against his.

"*Te amo.*" He captured her lips, joined them until they were both panting for breath. "*Te amo, Jodi. Te amo.*"

That one needed no translation. "I love you too," she replied softly.

The sweetness of Mark's declaration combined with the sensation of being so exquisitely filled, sandwiched between the two men, set her senses into overload. The fireworks sparkling at the edge of her vision exploded, a comet flaring across the sky. She came down from the heavens to hear Sam's deep groan as he filled her with liquid heat.

She collapsed against Mark's chest, her arms and legs shaking, unable to move. Sam withdrew and rolled to the side.

Before she'd regained her strength, a large hand slapped her tender behind.

"You're a very bad girl, Jodi," Sam said. "I only gave you permission to unzip Mark's fly, not blow him. And you definitely weren't supposed to fuck him yet."

But despite his stern manner, a broad grin lit his face. He leaned over and pressed a kiss on her cheek. "Thank you, sweet pea. Now, you'd better undo loverboy there before he starts to incinerate."

A promise in her smile, Jodi scrambled around and undid the restraint binding Mark's left ankle, then his right.

She lingered before undoing the arm restraints, teased his nipples, dipped one finger into his navel, curled her fingers around his cock and stroked the still-engorged head. Had he not completed when she and Sam had?

"Undo the damned wrist straps, will you?" he growled.

The moment she'd loosened the final clasp, Mark flipped Jodi onto the bed and held her in place with the weight of his body. Entered her. Claimed her.

Chapter Nine

Mark ploughed his cock into Jodi as if possessed, desperate to claim her back as his own, desperate to make her body forget what it felt like to have another man's cock stretching her, filling her.

"You're mine! *Only* mine," he growled.

When she wrapped her legs around his waist, welcoming him, his groans battled with the squeaks of the bed and the slap of his thighs against hers.

Embers burst into flame, rocketing down his spine. His balls tightened against his body, but he kept ramming into her until she screamed her release, something she hadn't done with Sam he noted with masculine pride.

Now. *Now.* His essence erupted, molten lava into a white-hot cavern, an explosion of love and anger and jealousy.

He collapsed on top of her, laying there for a few minutes, his breathing rough. Resting his forehead against hers, he stroked her face, crooning to her in Spanish knowing she wouldn't understand, and his tone gentle so she wouldn't know he cursed Sam, cursed himself. His touch trailed down her neck, stroked her shoulders, while his head dipped to kiss the reddened flesh of her breasts.

"*Te amo,*" he whispered. Had he said that earlier? He'd been thinking it. And had she said she loved him too? Not wanting to take the chance that she might not have understood, he repeated it in English. "I love you, Jodi."

"I love you too," she whispered.

He closed his eyes and said a silent prayer of thanks, and a vow that he'd never again allow another man to touch her the way Sam had. The way he'd invited Sam to.

Desperate to remove any trace of the other man from her skin, Mark touched everywhere Sam had touched. Everywhere Sam had tasted, Mark tasted. The memory of watching Sam's fingers on her soft flesh, of his cock stretching her pussy, and knowing he'd actually been the one to suggest it would be something he'd never forgive himself for.

Jodi tried to lift her hips but failed to move him. No way was he going to let her go until he'd made things right between them.

A flicker of pain crossed her face and she squirmed beneath him again.

"Aw, baby, did I hurt you?" He lifted his weight from her, but kept his arms stabbed into the mattress on either side of her, trapping her.

Her eyes fluttered open, a dazed and exhausted look filling them. "I think I'm lying on the nipple clamps."

Damn things. Mark reached beneath her. With a flick of his wrist, he withdrew the offending clamps and tossed them across the floor.

Mark rolled over and pulled her beside him, wrapping his arms around her in an iron grip. "Sam, this is en—"

He trailed off when he realized they were alone in the room, Sam nowhere in sight. Another stream of curses directed at both Sam and himself echoed off the walls.

"Mark?" Jodi said quietly, her eyes veiled as she glanced

down at his chest. "Did you want me to tell Sam no when he asked? Did I screw things up between us?"

He cursed himself again, softer this time, when he realized she thought he would blame her, that he might be angry that she'd agreed to Sam's suggestion. "I know it was my idea originally, but I couldn't..."

He averted his gaze, glancing at the mountain of pillows surrounding them. "When Sam and I discussed tonight's...entertainment...I thought I'd have no problem watching you with Sam. You know how I love to watch you play with yourself. And he wasn't lying about what we used to do back in college."

He took a deep breath and forced himself to look at her. Damn it, she still wasn't looking at him. Was she angry with him? Or had she found more pleasure with Sam?

"When it came down to it, to actually sharing you..." Words that usually flowed easily for him lodged in his chest. What if she thought about what he'd asked of her? What if she realized how he'd violated her trust by failing to protect her? "When Sam talked about penetrating your ass, when he touched you, this wave of anger started burning in my gut."

No shit, he'd felt like a caveman who wanted to grab her by the hair and carry her back to his cave. To beat Sam until his best friend lay bloodied and unmoving at his feet.

Her eyes squeezed shut as she turned her head away from him. "You *are* angry that I agreed."

He could have lost her tonight. He could still lose her.

He stroked the side of her face until her eyes opened and she slowly turned her head back to look at him. "No, babe. I'm not angry that you agreed. I could never be angry about that. It was my stupid idea, remember?"

"Not stupid," she said softly.

"I'm sorry. I'm so sorry for tonight and what I put you through."

She pushed away from him, shaking her head. "Sorry? For what? Because I have to tell you, I'm not."

"I behaved like a jerk. I should have asked you if you really wanted a threesome. I should have asked if there was anyone you wanted more. I should never have pressured you. I should... I..." His Adam's apple jerked as he swallowed, remembering the anger that had engulfed him when Sam had tied him to the bed, when he'd been forced to watch. "I was insane thinking I could share you."

"Ssshhh." She pressed a finger to his lips, silencing him. Her touch was soothing, as if she could sense his fear, his feelings of inadequacy. "You did give me a choice, remember? So did Sam. It's not like he hurt me or anything. We had a safe word—I could have used it any time."

He didn't want to remind her that a safe word was only good if the other person backed off. But Sam would have stopped—or he never would have trusted the bastard in the first place. Some of his anger bled away. And he had the rest of his life to make it up to her. For now, it was enough she forgave him.

For someone who had seen the worst life could throw at a person, she was so forgiving, so open. He was going to buy her the biggest diamond ring he could find. A diamond that would tell every other guy in the world "hands off, she's mine!"

If she'd wear it.

Chapter Ten

His stomach grumbling, Mark eased his arm from under Jodi and pulled the silk sheet over her. She squirmed, tugging her pillow closer beneath her but stayed asleep.

He picked up the remote Sam had used earlier and turned off the big screens one by one. Finding his blue jeans was more of a challenge—he ended up unearthing them from under the comforter they'd kicked off the bed. And his underwear was nowhere to be seen. Hell, he'd just go commando.

"Be right back, babe." A soft mewl escaped Jodi's lips when he bent down to brush a kiss across her forehead.

Barefoot, he padded from the room and climbed the stairs to the main level. A green-tinged light spilled from the office into the hallway. The creak of the leather chair, and a snap and hiss of a can opening told him where Sam had disappeared.

Time to settle that account.

His feet on the desk, ankles crossed, Sam leaned back in the chair, staring at the flat- screen television on the far wall, a Heineken in his hand. His leather pants had been traded in for a pair of grey fleece track pants, and, like Mark, he wore no shirt.

Muttering, Sam lifted the glass in a salute to the screen. The screen with an image of Jodi sleeping.

Mark cursed under his breath. Sam had been watching them this whole time?

With a snort of disgust, Mark walked into the room and flicked off the television. "And you accused me of being a voyeur."

Sam scratched idly at the scar on his chest. "Considering the glass house you live in, you shouldn't be tossing stones at me. 'Sides, I didn't have the sound turned up."

As if that made a difference.

Mark stared down at his friend. "Do you want to tell me why the fuck you thought it necessary to tie me up, *old buddy*?"

Sam placed the can on the desk, turned it until a dark circle of moisture imprinted on the blotter. Lifted it and placed it beside where it had been. Turned it again, making another circle.

"I did what I had to," he said finally.

Mark folded his arms across his chest. "You want to explain that?"

Another circle joined the others on the blotter. Then a fifth and a sixth. Sam finally lifted his gaze and met Mark's. "I didn't want to see you toss away a sure thing playing the games we played in college. You're not cut out for that lifestyle, Mark. And from what I've seen of her, neither's Jodi."

"If you thought it was wrong, you could have walked away. You could have not agreed in the first place."

Sam met his gaze evenly. "You said if I didn't help you, you'd find someone else. Couldn't take that chance."

"So you took control by tying me up."

Sam lifted the glass halfway to his lips then stopped. "Only way I could think of to prove my point."

"That having a ménage is a college game? Just how did

tying me up prove that?"

"My *point* was that you love that woman." Sam stabbed his hand through the air toward the television. "And she loves you. Didn't you see how she was looking at you when she asked you if she should continue? Shit, man, it was soul-deep love. Jodi's a one-man woman. She deserves a one-woman man. Someone who'll protect her. Love her. Who won't share her with anyone else. She's too damn special to have you offer her around to your friends so you can get off."

Mark snorted, but his anger evaporated as fast as a water drop on a hot griddle. He slumped into the chair on the opposite side of the desk. "You're right. I do love her. But I didn't realize that until tonight. What tipped you off?"

"Every time you said her name you got this goofy look on your face." Sam took another sip of his drink, then held up the can and glared at it, frowning. "But you were so damned determined to bring me in as your third, kept telling me it was just like 'the old days'. That you two were just partners having a little fun. You were trying too hard to convince yourself, ya know?

"And then tonight...when I touched her...I've never seen that look on your face before. You looked like you were ready to tear my head off."

"I was," Mark conceded.

"Yet you let me continue. Let her think you were cool with sharing her. And that was flat-out wrong." Sam set the can down and gave Mark a hard stare. "So I figured I had to do something to get through that thick skull of yours. Make you realize how good you got it."

Mark ran a hand over his scalp. "Yet this conscience of yours didn't stop you from fucking her, did it? You want to explain that one?"

One of Sam's shoulders pulled up in a halfhearted shrug. "It was all her choice. She could have used the safe word at any time. And don't forget that when I put the proposition to her, she asked you and you said—"

"I told her she could trust you. I let it go on." Mark scrubbed at his face, then dropped his hands into his lap. "I get your point. No more ménages. I don't think I could hold myself back if another man touched her. I'd probably rip his head off."

Sam closed his eyes and exhaled noisily. "Thank the good Lord above for that! She's a special lady." Sam leaned forward, planted his elbows on the desk. He pointed at Mark as if his fingers were a gun. "But you hear me, Mark, and you remember me well. If you mistreat her, if you fuck around on her, I'm gonna be on your ass like a hound dog on a hare. We straight?"

"You'd have to get in line," Jodie said from the doorway.

"Thanks for the offer, Sam, but if Mark ever fools around on me, I can take care of him myself." Jodi scissored her fingers together. "And I'll be more brutal than Lorena Bobbitt. If he fools around on me, Mark won't have any balls to tuck into his jockeys by the time I'm done with him."

Both men immediately crossed their legs.

Sam barked a laugh and pounded his fist on the desk so hard the phone jumped out of its base. "I think you've finally found someone who can keep you in line, ol' buddy."

"I wouldn't have it any other way." Mark grinned back. "Come over here, *Lorena*."

Jodi sauntered over to Mark, conscious of the hungry look in his eyes as he tracked her. She bent to kiss him but stopped an inch away from his lips, murmuring, "Oh, and by the way, if you think I'm going to invite another woman to our bed as a quid pro quo for tonight, I should warn you. It ain't gonna happen."

"I don't want anyone else." Mark pulled her onto his lap and nuzzled her neck.

"Man, if you two are going to get all mushy on me, I'm leavin'," Sam drawled then drained the remainder of his drink.

Jodi pulled away. "Don't leave, Sam. I want to thank you for what you did tonight." Color rose up her neck. "I mean, about tying Mark up—that *was* to make him jealous, wasn't it?"

He glanced away, as if unwilling to meet her gaze. "Yeah, well..."

"I appreciate what you did—especially since it could have backfired on you." She leaned over and kissed his cheek, then cocked her head and looked at him. "You know, I've got a friend I think you might like..."

He held up both his hands in mock surrender. "No thank you. I'm not desperate enough for a blind date." He grew serious as he glanced between them. "Look, if later on, down the road, you two decide you want a third in bed again, you call me, all right? And, Jodi, don't let Mark here ever force you to do something you don't want to do. He does, you call me and I'll pound some sense into his head."

"Thanks." She laughed and patted his hand. "You're a good friend, Sam."

"Man, how'd that sonuvabitch get so lucky in snatching you up?" He hung his head and shook it. When he lifted it, a sly smile crept over his broad face, lighting a twinkle in his eyes. "You sure you wouldn't consider coming to work for me back east? I'm always on the lookout for a good security consultant."

Jodi laughed and looped her arms around Mark's neck. "Nah, not a chance." She sobered. Sam's request reminded her of something that had been bugging her all night. "You know, Sam, I've been wondering..."

"Why am I thinkin' I should be worried?" Sam quirked an

eyebrow.

"I've been wondering why you left the combination to the safe where I could find it. You did that deliberately, didn't you? Were you testing my competence? Do you think I'm not good enough for your company?"

Mark swore under his breath. "No wonder you took that bet that you could crack it in under two minutes. You had the combination the whole time, you cheater."

"You know I never bet unless I'm absolutely sure I can win." She turned back to Sam. "I could have cracked the safe without the combination, you know."

Sam shrugged one shoulder. "Yeah, I know."

"So why make it easy on me? Why leave the combination where anyone could find it?"

The shoulder hitched up again. He crushed the can and tossed it in the trash. "You might not have found it."

She paused, watched him deliberately avoid her gaze. "There's something more here, isn't there?"

When he didn't answer, Mark straightened. "Sam? What are you hiding?"

Sam turned the chair sideways, eyed the door. "It's no biggie. Just forget about it, okay?" He opened the door to a small fridge built into the credenza. "Y'all want a drink? I've got ginger ale, beer, you name it."

"Sam?" Mark persisted.

"Oh, all right." Sam picked up another beer can then exchanged it for a bottle of Pellegrini. "It was part of a bet. Satisfied?"

Jodi turned to Mark and raised one brow in query. "Don't look at me, babe."

When both sets of eyes turned on him, Sam continued, "I

told my assistant to let you in without the usual security check so you'd buy into Mark's story about the place needing an upgrade in its security. But that woman was like a starving dog with a T-bone and wouldn't let it go until I explained exactly why I wanted to let you in."

Heat crept up Jodi's neck as she thought of the straitlaced assistant and what she might think if she knew what had really gone on that evening. She pressed her fingers to her mouth. "Please tell me you didn't tell her what you really had planned for tonight."

Sam scowled. "I do have some discretion, you know. I told her I was checking out the efficiency of Mark's employees as part of the merger agreement. Told her I'd challenged him to have you break into the safe."

"But that doesn't explain why you left the combination for me to find."

Sam eyed the door again, reminding her of how she'd felt trapped earlier that evening.

"Well, you see, I figured being a former cop and everything, you weren't a real girly girl." He slid down in his chair, his chin on his chest, then grasped the handles of his chair, until it groaned in protest. His next words came out in a rush. "I figured you wouldn't really clean things the way a maid would. Figured that you'd sort of dust around things, you know. But Sandy...Ms. Hallquist, she said if you were as good as Mark claimed, you'd be..." He shifted his weight again.

"That I'd be what?" Jodi asked, trying to hide the laughter caused by seeing the big man squirm in discomfort.

"That you'd be...you know...snoopy." The words left him in a rush.

"Snoopy?" Jodi laughed aloud. "Sam, I was reconnoitering for security flaws. Of course, I'd be snoopy!"

Obviously relieved that she wasn't offended, Sam let his shoulders drop and leaned back in his chair. "Sandy bet me that if she wrote the combination on the blotter—"

"—I'd find it." Jodi finished for him. "Which I wouldn't have unless I actually cleared the desk when I dusted."

"How much d'you lose?" Mark asked. Jodi could feel his muscles rippling as he tried not to laugh aloud.

Sam's cheeks turned bright red as he mumbled, "I have to enter myself in the annual bachelor auction to raise money for the homeless women's shelter."

Mark's laughter exploded, nearly unseating Jodi. "Oh, that's fucking perfect! Jodi, we have to go to that auction. I want to watch him squirm while all those women ogle his ass."

Sam looked up, a look of hope flickering in his eyes. "Hey, Jodi, maybe you could bid on me. You know, save a poor helpless bachelor from those biddies?"

Mark shook his head. "Not a chance! You made the bet, you suffer the consequences."

"I don't..." Jodi started, then hesitated as a thought struck her. But would her plan work, especially with the two huge egos these men had? "Maybe we could come to some arrangement."

"Jodi," Mark groaned. "Don't you dare buy into his 'poor bachelor' crap. I want to watch him strut his sorry ass down a runway like a frickin' supermodel—it's the perfect payback, babe."

Jodi bit her bottom lip. "I'll make the highest bid on you if you promise me something."

"What's that?" Sam eyed her as if she were a python ready to strike.

She pushed herself off Mark's lap, paced as she figured out exactly how to word her request so as not to offend either man.

Finally she stopped and took a deep breath. "It's about the merger. Mark loves Celada Security. He's worked real hard to get it where it is, and I'm afraid that when you take over—"

"Jodi," Mark said quietly. "Sam and I are good. You don't need to worry—"

Sam held up a hand, stopping Mark. "Let her have her say, Mark. She's just looking out for your interests. And I respect the hell out of her for that."

"If things don't work out," she continued, not wanting to meet Mark's eyes, "the two companies revert back to the way things are now. And you'll guarantee Hauberk won't compete for any contracts against Celada in Texas."

Sam opened a drawer and pulled out a thick folder, tossed it on the desk. "If it sets your mind at ease, sweet pea, Mark and I already had something similar written into the contract. Here's my copy—you can see for yourself."

Mark rested his hand over hers, his thumb gently stroking her wrist. "Considering he's the buying company, Sam didn't have to have that written in, babe. But he's the one who suggested it even before we put anything on paper."

Sam shrugged and glanced away as if uncomfortable with Mark's admission. "I treat my friends right."

"Thank you, Sam," Jodi said.

"Glad to see you lookin' out for him, sweet pea. I'd expect nothin' less from you." The chair creaked as Sam stood and stretched. "Oh, and, sweet pea, just in case you need to keep that old hound dog in line, the code to the safe room is seven-two-six-one-nine. Maybe you could give Mark a turn being tied to the posts some day. Remind him who's in charge."

He walked to the door then paused, a smile slowly blossoming across his face. "But you might want to phone first."

With a wink, he left.

She finally looked up at Mark, worried that perhaps she'd overstepped the boundaries, but saw no sign of irritation or anger on his face. "I didn't mean to stick my nose where it didn't belong. Are you mad at me?"

Mark shook his head. "No. As Sam said, you were looking out for me." He laced his fingers with hers and tugged her back onto his lap. "Kind of nice to know you worry about me like that. Besides, as Hauberk's new vice president of Western Operations, it's a reasonable concern."

"Vice president?" A thrill shot through her at the title until she remembered Mark's daily frustrations dealing with employees who were late or failed to show up at critical times. His anger when he caught several operatives smoking joints while on duty. And the mountains of paperwork that covered his desk. "Does that mean I have to sit behind a desk shuffling papers all day?"

Mark snorted. "As if that'll ever happen." When she tweaked a handful of chest hair, he sighed. "All right, there will be some paperwork involved. But you can hire an assistant if you need one. It also means you'll get to boss the guys around even more than you do now."

"I'm not bossy!"

He raised one eyebrow. "You just bullied a guy who's six foot six and weighs two eighty buck naked about the merger. That wasn't bossy?"

"That was..." she walked her fingers up his chest, "...a negotiation. On behalf of someone I love."

His hands slipped underneath the bottom of her shirt, cupped her breast with his palms, his thumbs brushing over the sensitive tips. "Hmm. I love hearing you say that."

She leaned into his touch, eyes closing. Talented fingers, she thought for what had to be the umpteenth time that night. “What? That I negotiated for you?”

“No, that you love me. You’ve never said that before.”

The distinctive sound of a Harley revved outside. Jodi rushed to the window just in time to see Sam tugging on his helmet. “I knew I’d heard a motorcycle! But how’d he get in without me seeing it?”

She glanced back and saw Mark’s lips clamp together, a telltale twitch at the side betraying his urge to smile.

“You! You came with him, didn’t you?” She poked him in the chest and thought back to when he’d arrived, and what he’d done. “And then you deliberately distracted me from watching the monitors, didn’t you? With that stupid vibrating egg!”

“Didn’t take much effort,” Mark said. He stood behind her, wrapping his arms about her waist as they watched Sam glance back at the house. He gave a salute toward them, then roared down the driveway.

Chapter Eleven

Mark turned her away from the window until she faced him, then kissed her, his lips brushing over hers in a featherlight touch. "*Te amo.*"

Jodi wrapped her arms about his neck, pulled him closer until her breasts brushed his chest. "I love you too."

Not knowing what was at the bottom of the chasm he was about to leap into, he teetered on the edge. He hated the strange feeling of fear curling in his bowels. But there was no going back after tonight, there was no way he could let her walk away with someone else.

She nestled her head in the crook of his shoulder, rested her hand on his chest. Everything about her felt so right.

"Babe? I, uh, have something to ask you." He swallowed hard. She'd said she loved him, but that didn't mean she wanted to marry him. *What if she said no?*

She pulled back to look at him, her eyes wide, almost fearful, held her body still. "What?"

He took a deep breath and leapt into his future. "Will you marry me?"

Jodi stiffened in his arms. "M-marry? Marry you?" The words seemed forced, as if they'd stuck in her throat.

Somewhere in the back of his mind, he'd wanted her to

throw her arms about his neck and shout, “Yes, yes, yes! Of course, I’ll marry you.” Instead her hold on him loosened and blank shock filled her eyes. The bright light that he’d hoped would be his future turned out to be a heat-seeking missile racing toward him, its target his heart.

“I still want you to be vice president of Western Operations, whether you say no or not,” he said quickly, wondering if she thought her answer might be tied to the promotion. “Sam and I discussed it already. I just hoped... I want to...” He stumbled on, unable to stop himself from babbling, knowing he was sounding like an idiot. “I love you and want to marry you.”

She laughed, a half-hysterical sound he’d never heard from her before. Her head dropped onto his shoulder as her body rippled. Was she crying? Worse, she was laughing. No. Giggling!

“You...you...you want to m-m-marry me!” Her giggles reached an almost hysterical quality.

He’d bared his soul to her, asked her to marry him and she was giggling? His arms dropped as the missile hit its target and shredded his flesh, his soul. “I didn’t think it was so funny.”

“Oh, M-Mark,” she choked out from behind the fingers she’d pressed over her mouth. “I’m sorry, I’m not laughing at you. I’m laughing at me.”

Sure didn’t feel that way.

“You see, tonight”—her giggles trailed off into a sigh—“tonight, when I was waiting for you in the van? I thought...I thought you were trying to brush me off, to dump me.”

He felt his jaw drop. Dump her? After all he’d gone through to arrange this evening? Would he ever understand how women thought?

“Why?” he finally managed to splutter.

“Because you’ve been so distant lately.” She held up her

hand when he started to protest. "It was like you were trying to avoid me. I-I thought maybe you'd gotten tired of me. I thought maybe you thought it was time to move on."

He scrubbed his hand through his hair. "I'm sorry—I've been busy arranging this evening with Sam, and hammering out the details of the merger. I never meant for you to feel like I was ignoring you."

"I know." She released a breath and her voice wavered. "No, I didn't know. I just kept remembering that agreement we made that either of us could walk away at any time, no questions asked."

He saw pain flicker through her eyes, realized she was remembering how she'd been treated by past lovers. Cursed himself for forgetting that beneath the tough exterior Jodi showed everyone else was a sensitive woman who needed reassurance that she could be herself without fear of rejection. He ran a finger along her jaw, marveling at how others didn't realize her tough shell was just an act. "I've just been distracted. I'm sorry. If I wasn't interested I would have told you straight out. I wouldn't have just walked away."

"I wasn't sure what you'd do," she said softly, not realizing how much it hurt him that she might think he could treat her so callously. "I figured you just might not know how to tell me. After all, we did agree that we wouldn't...you know..."

"Fall in love?" He captured her hand with his, pressed a kiss to her palm. "Jodi, I've never felt like this"—he moved her hand to his chest, flattened her palm over his heart—"about any other woman. Ever. I love you. And I want to marry you. Will you marry me, Jodi?"

She looked up at him, her bright blue eyes filled with tears. "Yes. Oh, Mark, of course I'll marry you."

He released the breath he'd been holding and enfolded her

within the circle of his arms, held tight, realized he was shaking with the fear that had engulfed him that she might say no.

When he nuzzled his nose against the side of her neck, he frowned. He could still smell a trace of cigar—of Sam—in her hair. He silently cursed himself again for letting another man touch her, while thanking Sam for forcing the issue, for forcing him to acknowledge how much he loved the woman in his arms. His grip loosened from about her and he stepped back.

"Come with me." He held out his hand, waiting until she put her palm into his.

Neither spoke while they walked down the hall. Mark led her up the stairs and to the bathroom they'd used earlier. When she'd brought him there earlier, she'd not wanted to let Sam between them yet. He wondered if she realized he felt the same way now.

He reached into the shower and turned on the water. When he was satisfied with the temperature he turned back to her. He grasped the hem of her T-shirt and pulled it over her head and discovered she wore no bra.

"So beautiful," he murmured. He cupped her breasts with his palms, bent his head and licked, savored.

Jodi arched, pressing her breasts deeper into his mouth. Her hands rested lightly on his shoulders, her thumbs caressing the sides of his neck. "Thank you for giving me a birthday I'll never forget." She chuckled. "It's not a story we can ever tell our children, but—"

"Children?" Mark breathed. His balls retracted in a painful clench. How had tonight gone from his planned night of debauchery to a discussion about marriage *and* kids? "You want kids?"

She jerked back, the smile dropping from her face. "Don't you?"

"Yeah, yeah, I want kids," he quickly assured her while wondering if he did. His eyes dropped to her belly, imagined it swollen with his child. Imagined having a little boy he could play catch with. Maybe a little girl he could carry around on his shoulders. Yeah, he could do that. "Yeah, I want kids."

Maybe that would stop his younger brother José's ceaseless bragging about how he'd given their parents the first grandchild. Like the twerp had done it himself. His chest swelled as he pictured announcing to his brothers that he'd given their parents the first grand*son*—no, grandsons!—in the family. "Two. At least two."

Her smile returned. And with it his world returned to an even keel, although spinning slightly faster than it had been before the evening had started.

"Let's start with one and see how we do from there, okay?" Jodi wrapped her arms about his neck and pulled him close. "But it may take some practice first."

"Practice. Yeah, practice is good." He pressed her against the tile wall. "For instance, I need lots of practice kissing you."

"Mmm." She turned her head, captured his lips with hers. What seemed like an hour later, they both came up for air. "What else do we need to practice?"

She caught her breath when she saw the dark embers deep in his eyes flare into wildfire. Why had she thought he didn't love her? It was there plain in his eyes. It was in his calloused fingers as he cupped her breasts, rolled her nipples between his fingers with a delicious pressure. In his voice, the trace of Spanish accent betraying the depth of his emotion as he spoke, "If we're going to have children, you're going to want to breastfeed them, right?"

She moaned as warm breath and warmer lips caressed her, teased her, tasted her. Cool air touched her bare skin when he pushed her jeans to the floor, his tongue never stopping its homage to her breasts. When he shifted, forcing her to arch her back, she dug her fingers into his shoulders and hung on. Hung on to the man she loved. Who loved her.

His clothes abandoned on the floor beside hers, Mark carried her into the shower, held her beneath the pulsing streams of water and began to wash her, his soapy hands lathering her shoulders, her breasts, her belly.

No inch of her escaped his attention. Where downstairs his lovemaking had been with a fierce desperation, now he took the time to caress her, to worship every part of her body. Every place he touched ignited until her blood boiled and her skin was ready to burst into flames.

When his fingers dipped deep into her heat, she arched into his touch. The rhythmic pounding of the shower on her skin was no match for the conflagration he fanned deep within her.

By the time he slid into her, Jodi was sure the smoke alarms would go off and the fire trucks would scream down the lane.

The water had long since gone cold, and they'd moved from the shower to the bed when Mark wrapped an arm around Jodi, tugging her back against him.

"I'm thinking we should look for a house in the Mid Cities, maybe Grapevine. One with lots of bedrooms." His hand drifted to her belly. "And then I'm going to install a security system rivaling Fort Knox. After all, I can't have anyone else getting their hands on my private property."

Deliberate Deceptions

Dedication

To N and J, who shared their fears and grief with me to help bring Chad and Lauren's story alive. To my husband and sons for making dinner too many nights to count, and for learning how to corral the dust bunnies by themselves (even though they may not realize they've now set a precedent).

Chapter One

April 2001

Life couldn't get any better. Chad Miller soaked in the sight of his baby daughter in her mother's arms. Even from where he stood in the doorway, he could see Emily's lips drawn into a bow, moving as if she was still suckling. The light from the bedside lamp limned Lauren, gilding her hair that spilled over her shoulder. Had any man ever been so lucky?

"Hey, babe," he said softly so he wouldn't disturb Emily.

Lauren turned her head and gave him a smile worthy of a Madonna. "I didn't hear you come in. Everything go okay?"

"It went down perfect. We got the guy." Pride swelled in him as she carefully placed Emily in her cradle beside their bed. "Got some other good news too. You're looking at the Bureau's newest Supervisory Special Agent."

With a squeak of joy, Lauren ran toward him, heedless of the way the light turned her nightgown transparent. His cock hardened as he watched the V of her legs open and close with each step she took. No, not a Madonna. A siren. With a body to tempt any man. Except he was the only man who got to explore her sensuality.

He wrapped his arms about her and held her tight. God, he was so lucky to have them both. "I love you, baby."

She pulled back and gave him a cocky grin. "That's just because you hope to get lucky tonight."

"I'm lucky every night. Ever since you came into my life."

"I love you too. And I'm so proud of you." She kissed him, her lips soft on his, her tongue demanding entrance. He drew a deep breath, reveling in the lingering scent of Lauren's shampoo mixed with a hint of the baby powder she'd used on Emily. Her pelvis ground against his erection until he broke off the kiss with a groan.

Okay, so life could get better in one way. He glanced at the cradle as he stroked Lauren's behind, trailing one finger down the cleft in the center. "Em down for the night?"

"Mmm-hmm." The edges of Lauren's eyes crinkled with her smile. She pulled back to look at him, the warm brown irises glowing like a twenty-year-old scotch in the dim light. Then he noticed the dark circles beneath them.

With a frown, he rubbed a thumb over her jaw, loving how she rested her cheek in his palm. "You're tired, babe. Why don't we arrange a babysitter for tomorrow night? Go out, indulge in some grown-up games for a change."

His balls ached at the thought that he'd not be able to celebrate right damned then. He'd been half-hard ever since the take-down. The adrenaline hadn't eased since he'd received news of his promotion and he'd been looking forward to this all night.

She cast a glance of her own at the cradle. "I'm all right, as long as we can be where I can keep an eye on her." Her hand drifted down his abdomen to smooth the fabric straining over his erection. The tiny dimple that only appeared on the right side of her smile deepened. "Besides, I think we need to take care of this bad boy soon or you're not going to sleep tonight."

"Not without a hand job in the shower." He released a slow

breath when she unzipped his fly and stroked his cock. His fingers threaded through her hair, loving the feel of the silken strands against his skin. “Hell, you keep that up, I’m going to come right here.”

With another hmm, Lauren sank to her knees. Two seconds later, his pants were around his ankles, his cock bobbing inches away from her face.

Warm breath was quickly followed by the moist heat of her mouth as she licked his crown. Her lips closed around his shaft in one swallow, wrenching a groan from him. They’d been together long enough they didn’t need words; she knew instinctively what he liked. He tightened his grip on her hair when she cupped his balls, causing a familiar tingle at the base of his spine.

An animal-like growl rose in his throat as his seed pulsed into the warmth of her mouth. The sensation of her swallowing it around his spasming cock nearly had his knees buckling. Her tongue swiped around the head, licking the last drops of his come as delicately as a cat licking the last of a bowl of cream. She sat back on her heels with a look of satisfaction.

“Come here, babe. Let me take care of you now.” He pulled her to her feet and caressed her mound. His fingers parted her soft folds, sliding through the moisture. He’d never understood why a woman would get off giving head, but Lauren had always been aroused whenever she’d sucked him off.

She buried her face in the crook of his neck, her hips undulating her clit against his fingers. “It’s all right, don’t worry about me.”

The hell with that. He walked her backward until the back of her knees hit the bed. Her head turned, seeking the cradle, but he captured her lips with his. “She’s fine.”

Once Lauren was horizontal, he banded her wrists and

hauled them above her head. “Don’t move.”

She started to argue but he kissed her again, cutting off whatever she was about to say. They were both breathless by the time he pulled away. “Don’t. Move.”

He left her there while he opened the bedside table and chose a set of leather wrist restraints. It had been almost a year since he’d let himself take her the way he liked, the way she liked. Since Lauren had first told him she suspected she might be pregnant. He’d been gentle each time they’d made love, ensuring nothing he did would harm her or their baby. But tonight. Tonight there were no excuses not to indulge themselves.

Without being asked, she held up her hands. He kissed the tender skin on the inside of her wrists before he fastened the cuffs around them, then attached the restraints to the headboard. Free to explore at his leisure, he traced a finger around one areola. They were darker, bigger than they’d been before her pregnancy. God, he found it so amazing that she could give life to their child, and such pleasure to him.

Straddling her, he leaned down and kissed her mouth, pouring all the love she’d given him back to her. Beneath him, she shuddered, her hips undulating. His hand drifted over her belly, goose bumps raising wherever he touched. He slid his fingers between her creamy lips and plunged into her pussy. Lauren moaned into his mouth while grinding her clit against his palm.

He broke off the kiss. “Easy, babe. You’ll get what you want in a minute.”

His head dropped to her neck and he feathered kisses down her shoulder. He took his time, paying attention to her breasts, to her belly, to the silvery lines she’d worried made her look ugly. Would she ever believe him when he told her that he loved her stretch marks? That to him they were proof of the love they'd shared? Of their daughter.

He settled between her thighs. Her whole body trembled when his tongue touched her clit. His cock hardened, and his balls ached at the taste of her honey. He drove her up to the brink, backed off, then drove her up again until her juices coated his chin and she was begging him to let her come. His fingers working deep inside her, he lifted his head. Her cheek rested on the pillow, her shoulder-length hair a golden halo in the light. "Look at me, babe."

Her head turned as if it were a struggle to move. He watched her eyes unfocus as he sucked her clit. Her lips parted as she panted in short, hard bursts. He flicked his tongue against the nerve endings once, twice, with the strength he knew would tip her over the edge. The long expanse of her neck arched cutting off his view as her pussy spasmed around his fingers.

Before her muscles stopped their fluttering, he surged into her. Although they both tried to be quiet, he couldn't stop his groan. Damn, her pussy was still taut, clutching his cock with a welcoming warmth, the lingering remains of her orgasm driving him insane.

Lauren wrapped her legs around his waist and nailed his ass with her heels, pulling him even deeper. "Please," she whispered.

He closed his eyes and stopped moving, summoning his control over his need to plunge into her over and over, to use her hard and fast. He slid his hands beneath her silky, firm globes, adjusting the angle before withdrawing, inch by slow inch. Just as slowly as he'd withdrawn, he pressed back in, until she was whimpering, her body shaking with need.

No matter how rigid his control, soon he was flexing his

hips until the bed frame bounced against the wall, burying every inch of himself into the most sublime place on earth. The sensation of her heated channel rippling tight around his cock shattered his restraint. His balls tight to his body, he buried his face between her breasts and let his need for Lauren, his pride and his love, pour into her.

His body sagged on her until he gathered the strength to roll over. He reached up and undid the restraints. As soon as she was free, Lauren curled inside his embrace. A breath, maybe two, and she was asleep, her lips parted, her eyelashes long on her cheeks.

He started to rouse her, wanting to take her again, but the circles beneath her eyes stopped him. Emily hadn't been waking for the two-o'clock feeding for a month now, but Lauren still seemed exhausted even though she usually managed at least six hours uninterrupted sleep most nights. He stroked her breast, thumbing the heavy nipple that beaded beneath his touch. Hell, he chastised himself, she was feeding a child, that would be enough to make anyone tired.

He glanced over Lauren's shoulder and saw the gentle rise and fall of Emily's chest as she slept. She'd flipped over onto her stomach, a trick that left him inordinately proud. Why he should be so proud of something every child had to learn to do, he couldn't say. Soon she'd be sitting up by herself, then standing, then walking. Talking. Calling him Daddy.

God, he couldn't wait for that day.

Lauren shifted in her sleep with a quiet murmur and he lay down again, holding her in his arms. Life really was good, he thought as he drifted off to sleep.

And awoke to Lauren screaming.

Chapter Two

Present Day

Lauren stepped from the Brigade's jet onto the tarmac, glad to be standing on firm earth after being in the air for almost ten hours. The smog-shrouded Washington Monument across the Potomac drew her attention, a calming beacon saluting her return. Would its people be as welcoming?

A sleek, black stretch Humvee limo sat with its engine running less than thirty feet away. The driver got out, his windbreaker unbuttoned to allow easy access to the weapon he always wore. After a quick check of the area, he opened the back door, allowing the devil himself to step out.

Cooper Davis straightened his French cuffs and smoothed his perfectly pressed Armani suit before nodding to his driver. Anyone meeting him for the first time might buy his cover as an unassuming businessman, intent only on making a killing on Wall Street; she knew better. He strolled across the pavement with confidence and nonchalance, as if he were about to greet an old lover. Something he'd once suggested. To this day she hadn't decided if it had been a test or a sincere proposition.

She turned her face when he bent down to kiss her so his lips brushed her cheek. One dark eyebrow quirked up at her evasion. "Welcome back, Lauren."

"I'm done, Cooper. I want out." Saying the words both

soothed the jumbled thoughts in her brain while setting free the butterflies in her stomach.

"I figured you'd say that." He gestured toward the Humvee. "Let's sit inside while we discuss your future, shall we?"

She followed him to the Humvee, taking a seat facing him so she could read his facial expressions. As soon as the door closed behind them, sealing them into Cooper's bulletproof, soundproof world, he leaned forward. "There's a problem you should know about before you start planning on retiring."

Problem to Cooper could mean anything from a paperwork snafu to the start of the next world war. From the way every cell in her body went on alert, it was probably more the latter than the former. "I was right, wasn't I? Someone in the Brigade was behind those attacks."

"Yes." He stared out the window, his eyes narrowed. "Frank Harris."

She sucked in her breath. Of all the Brigade's operatives, Harris was both their best marksman and their best tracker. He was also currently the most unstable.

"From what we can gather, he discovered it was you who filed the complaint. He's declared war on you, Lauren."

"I need to leave then. Find a bolt hole. New York. L.A. San Francisco. Somewhere I can get lost in a crowd."

Cooper nodded slowly. "It might work. But it's also possible that Harris will try to get at you through people you care about, Lauren. What'll you do then?"

People she cared about? She'd long been estranged from her only sister and her mother had died a decade ago. Which left... "Chad?"

"It's a distinct possibility."

No. It couldn't be. Hadn't she screwed up Chad's life

enough without making him the target of a vengeful ex-CIA operative? "But we're divorced. We've been divorced for almost seven years now."

"Harris was there when you and Thalia had that blow-up a couple months ago. He knows you didn't want the divorce, and he knows you still love Chad. It's possible he'll use Chad as a way to control you or hurt you."

"I never said I love Chad." She'd never admitted it in words but... She thought back, desperate to remember exactly what had been said that day. Was the fight itself enough to tell Harris—and everyone else who'd overheard—how she felt?

"Maybe not in so many words that day, but you did discuss it with Doc Brewer at your last assessment, didn't you?"

"Those files are private." Her eyes widened at his implication. "Harris read them?"

He nodded. "We just discovered someone accessed them last month. We can only assume it was Harris."

"You've read them too," she whispered.

"I'm in charge of the unit, Lauren. I read everyone's reports. But I didn't need a report to tell me you still had strong feelings for Chad." He chuckled darkly. "Luckily for you, the way you insisted on not being stationed back here in the States led everyone else to assume it was out of hatred for Chad, not love."

"I didn't want to come back because I wanted to avoid Thalia." Not to mention avoiding the park where she used to take Emily for walks. The hospital where she was born. The Mall where Chad had proposed on the steps of the Lincoln Monument. The condo they had worked so hard to buy that had later become their prison thanks to the media frenzy after Chad had defied Bureau protocol.

"I didn't know what Thalia had done until you two had that fight, Lauren," Cooper said quietly. "If I had, I would have said something sooner."

"Do you know what she did?" She blew out her breath in a slow stream, forcing her shoulders down.

"I know that she was the one who recommended you to Sir Ian when he was running the Brigade and arranged for you to stay out of the country. And I know she hired the solicitor in London so it would look to Chad as if you were seeking the divorce, not him." He tilted his head as he observed her. "Am I right in assuming she's the one who recommended you stay at Tranquil Pastures?"

"Yes. Damn it, I should have flown back here and talked to him face-to-face instead of believing her or that damned lawyer. I had no idea she hated me that much."

"It's not that she hated you, it's that she loves her brother over everything else. And why wouldn't you believe her? What reason would you have had to suspect she was lying when she told you Chad was with someone else, that they were living together?"

Not to mention how he'd never replied to any of the letters she'd sent him that first year or the ones from Dr. Maudsley either. Had Thalia found some way to prevent Chad from getting them? Did it matter anymore?

She closed her eyes in an effort to calm the maelstrom raging inside. At her anger at Thalia for interfering. Her disgust at not discovering the deception for all these years burned with glowing embers of long-simmering resentment. Her rage against Harris burned brightly, its flames licking hungrily at her patience

"Maybe she wasn't lying. Maybe she just saw the inevitable. We were already in counseling. Neither of us handled Emily's death well. With Chad facing the inquiry and all that press...he was better off without having me distracting him." She settled back in her seat.

She'd mourned the loss of her marriage as much as she'd mourned her daughter.

"So you're not interested in resolving any issues between you and Chad? Seeing if there's still a chance of having a relationship with him?"

God, don't give her hope. It would only be torn from her the way it had been before. She couldn't take losing Chad again. "Just how would we do that after all this time?"

Cooper laid out his plans quickly and succinctly, hope rising in her soul with each step he revealed. The hopes mingled with the thought that he was crazy. Or brilliant. Maybe both. His plan would keep her safe, as well as Chad. Plus, it would let her finally see Chad again, to find out if he hated her for being so weak that she'd walked away when he'd needed her most. No, not walked. She'd run away with her tail tucked between her legs. Cooper was right—she needed to see Chad face-to-face one last time. If for no other reason, to apologize. And explain.

Icy fingers of fear doused the flames. What if Cooper's plan didn't work? He leaned forward. "If you're worried about Thalia interfering again, she's been taken out of the equation. She and Spencer are staying with a friend of mine who can keep them safe until Harris is found."

"What about Sam Watson? How are you going to explain about me considering he doesn't know about the Brigade?" There were so many stumbling blocks to his plan, and Hauberk's owner wasn't the least of them. If he decided not to help, he'd move heaven and hell to keep her and Chad apart. Maybe he'd even known Thalia's plan from the start.

"Ed Weir is on his way to Hauberk as we speak. That's why we're waiting here on the tarmac. If everything goes as planned, you'll be getting back on the plane and flying off to wherever

Hauberk plans on stashing you. Somewhere Chad will be your captive audience."

Would it be possible to undo the ten years—more—of damage that distance and ill feelings had wrought between them? He hadn't answered her question about whether Sam knew about his involvement with the Brigade.

"You'll have that second chance at your marriage you told Brewer you wanted."

Did she dare hope that? Or was it too late? Had too much time built a wall between them? Would it be too high for her to scale, to tear down and rebuild their marriage? Could they stay alive long enough to find out?

The last invoice stamped and initialed, Chad placed it on top of the rest in his out box with a sigh. Damned paperwork. It didn't matter how much he signed today, there'd be a whole new pile waiting for him tomorrow.

He opened his top drawer and stared at the silver-framed photograph. Emily with her beautiful, toothless grin, her chubby fist clutching her favorite stuffed bear. Lauren holding Emily, her expression bright and proud. Who knew when that picture had been taken, less than a month later the chuckles and smiles would change to anguished sobs that, to this day haunted his dreams.

The day after he'd been served with the divorce papers, he packed the picture away. The following day he'd retrieved it. He'd compromised by tucking the frame where he could look at it without anyone else knowing. At least he'd managed to wean himself down to looking at it only a couple times a day instead of several times an hour.

"Got a minute?" Hauberk's owner, Sam Watson, filled the

doorway. Only the sharpness of his gaze belied the casual way he leaned against the frame. Sam probably knew about the picture and its hiding spot so why the hell did he bother with the deception?

Even so, Chad slid the drawer shut and nodded. "Of course."

Sam closed the door behind him, then settled himself into one of the visitor's chairs opposite Chad, the leather creaking beneath his weight.

They discussed the various reports that had come in the night before, the state of the new office Sam was setting up in Seattle, and a half dozen other unimportant topics that had Chad responding by rote. While Sam droned on, Chad rolled his pen in his fingers. The light fractured on the brushed gold, the engraved initials so worn they were barely legible. His sister Thalia had given it to him—crap, fifteen years ago. The day he'd graduated the FBI's academy.

Sam pulled a cigar from his pocket and eyed it. "Damn, I wish I'd never promised Sandy I wouldn't smoke during office hours."

"You're the boss. Tell her it's your office and light up anyway." He suppressed the smile that threatened to break out imagining their assistant's righteous indignation. Sandy would have Sam quivering in a corner in a heartbeat.

As he'd expected, Sam snorted. "Yeah, right. Then she'd move all my files on my computer, or rename them so I couldn't find anything."

"More likely she'd serve you one of those flowery teas she likes. Force you to drink it in front of Jimbo Williams." They both knew how one of their wealthiest and most influential clients judged a man by how he took his coffee.

"Shee-it. I can hear him now." Sam adopted a nasal tone

pitched two octaves higher than his usual bass. "*No real man puts pansy-assed creamer or sugar in his coffee, Sammy, not if they've got a dick between their legs. Don't send some pinky-wavin' tea drinker to guard me either. You might as well cut off my nuts and call me Sally.*"

Controlling the smile at Sam's perfect imitation of their client, Chad carefully placed the pen so it lined up with his day planner. "Why are you here, Sam?"

"What do you mean?"

"You didn't come here to discuss Jimbo Williams." He lined the day planner up at perfect angles to the blotter that was precisely in line with the desk edge. "Or the new office in Seattle. Or how the newbie screwed up last night." He looked pointedly at Sam. "By the way, I will talk with him about that, not you."

Sam grimaced and slid the cigar back in his pocket. "A little birdy told me that on Sunday the Post is running a 'where are they now' feature and you're one of their targets."

His balance tilted as if someone had hit him with a sledgehammer. "Aw fuck, Sam, you know they've played that angle before. Hell, the fires were still burning in the Pentagon when that headline hit."

"Yeah, I know." Sam had been mentioned often enough but, according to press reports, he'd been following orders like a mindless robot. "I also know of the cases our office was handling back then, none involved any of those terrorists and there's no way your decision was responsible for the attacks. You know the press. They've got to have their story and they're ready to use any angle they can to boost their sales."

Chad tilted his head to one side then the other in an effort to loosen the tightening neck muscles. "So we wait it out. It'll be a headline for the weekend, then some other scandal will erupt and they'll move on. Face it, Sam, it's a non-event. I'm old news."

"Maybe so, but why don't you take a few days off yourself? Take a vacation. Get out of Washington."

Chad blinked before he caught himself. "You think I'm going to run out when you and Rosie are due to leave for Hawaii in—" he checked his watch, "—nine hours? Someone has to stay and look after this place."

"Yeah, about that." Though Sam didn't look away, he shifted in his seat as if he were uncomfortable. "We've rearranged things. Looks like I'm gonna be around for a while."

Rosie had been fretting for weeks about finally meeting Sam's mother but there's no way in hell she would have cancelled out. So why...shit. Sam wanted to distance Hauberk from Chad's sullied reputation. After all he'd done to help build up the company until it was one of the biggest on the eastern seaboard?

"You think I'm a detriment to the company."

"Shee-it, no." Sam's hand drifted to his pocket, seeking the cigar again. With a curse, he lowered his hand, his fingers flexing, restless. In other words, yes, but he couldn't admit it.

"Do you want my resignation? Because if you do, it'll be on your desk in thirty minutes. You want to buy me out too?"

"No, I don't want your resignation or to buy you out. You're half of Hauberk, for fuck's sake."

"But you don't want me around the office for a while, do you? You don't want our clients reminded of why Hauberk got started. Because of my fuck-up."

Sam stood and leaned over the desk, planting his fists on either side of the blotter. "I suggested you get away because you're more than my partner, you're my friend, damn it. I suggested you get away because I hate to see you hounded by the press, enduring the crap they fling at you. You took the heat for me back then, at least let me take some heat for you now."

"I deserved the heat. And those reporters?" He flung an arm toward the window. "They were right. If you and Jill had been available for another case, it would have freed up two other agents who might have freed up two other agents somewhere else who might have tumbled onto the 9/11 conspiracy." He played his trump card. "Maybe Jill would still be alive."

Sam's expression went blank, and his voice lowered, a sure warning sign he was approaching meltdown. "That's a low blow, even for you. Especially for you."

"But it's true, isn't it? I'm the one who sent you two undercover without authorization. If you hadn't been following my orders, Jill wouldn't have been killed, and you wouldn't have ended up flat on your back in hospital with a bullet a half inch from your heart."

"Maybe Jill would still be alive, but Thalia—your own sister, damn it—would be dead. Butchered." Sam folded his arms across his chest, a sure sign he was settling in for a fight he didn't intend to lose. "Who knows how many others Vandeburg would have killed that night? Or gone on to kill another night if I hadn't taken him out?"

Even hearing that man's name was like having someone twist a knife in his guts. Goddamn the bastard. How many people—living and dead—had David Vandeburg destroyed? Was he still destroying?

"It was the MPDC's responsibility to catch him." He was relieved that his voice stayed level as he recited the mantra his superiors had chanted right before they'd taken his FBI badge and let the door hit his ass on the way out.

"We both know they were only doing drive-bys. They

wouldn't have caught him that way. You think I haven't gone over your decision a million times? Wondered if maybe those headlines were right? You made a decision to catch a killer when everyone else turned their backs because of who he was killing. Because of you, we stopped a serial killer."

"The point is I went against orders. I deserve the heat, Sam. Every fucking bit of it." His voice was flat, betraying none of the rage that roiled in his chest. Thalia might not be dead, but she'd never walk again. He'd failed to protect her despite everything he'd done.

A knock on the door had them both turning around. The head of Hauberk's International group, Troy McPherson, strolled in, looking grim, followed by another man Chad didn't recognize. "Sam, Chad, I'd like you to meet Ed Weir. Ed's got an employee who needs a safe house."

"Nice to meet you, Ed." Sam rose to shake Weir's hand. "Why don't you take a seat and we'll work out the details."

Weir sprawled on the couch instead of taking the leather visitor's chair Sam pushed his way. He hitched one ankle onto his knee. "As McPherson said, I've got a business associate who needs to be kept somewhere safe until we can find the bugger who's threatening her."

Sam hitched his chair around and settled back into it. "Then you've come to the right place."

Chad let Sam run with the company patter while he composed a note to his net wizard Dan to dig up everything he could on Weir. Once the email had been sent, he sat back and assessed their newest client. South African from his accent. Weir's alert gray eyes behind wire-framed glasses assessed his surroundings with the attentiveness Chad expected from his agents. The gaze stopped briefly at the holster beneath Chad's arm before rising to his face.

Interesting and commendable. Many of their clients couldn't have told him what color suit he'd been wearing after talking with them for an hour.

Salt and pepper hair that had once been sandy brown had been clipped so it was no longer than an inch anywhere on his head. There was more gray in the neatly trimmed goatee. Forty perhaps, give or take a couple years. He'd been taller than Troy when they were standing in the doorway which pegged him at six foot two, give or take an inch. A hundred-and-eighty pounds, though that was probably generous.

"I own a few mining ventures back home." Gold or diamonds? Chad wondered. No wedding ring, but a heavy gold link bracelet on his right wrist and a Rolex—one of the Oyster models without diamonds—confirmed Weir had a healthy bank account. Wouldn't a diamond mine owner wear their own product? Gold then perhaps.

"A few months ago, I came to believe we had a mole in the company, someone who might be looking to steal a device we've been working on that should help us find new lodes. So I hired the woman I want you to guard to do some discreet investigation."

"Let me guess—she kicked over some rocks and found a snake?" Sam leaned forward, planting his elbows on his knees.

"Yes. We know who the mole is—and they've been neutralized. Unfortunately the person the informant was selling the information to has taken it personally."

Neutralized? Chad frowned. In his business that meant they'd been killed.

Sam didn't seem as concerned about that line of thought. "You said there have been threats. What type?"

Weir toyed with the hem of his pants on the ankle he'd hitched over his knee. "Someone tossed a Molotov cocktail through her flat's window last Tuesday night. She got out, a little singed but no worse for wear." Chad figured that was an understatement but kept his peace as Weir continued. "My government recommended she return to the States while they investigated the attack. Since I had meetings here this week, I accompanied her."

Troy, who had been leaning against the wall listening silently up to this point, grabbed the remaining vacant chair. "It didn't work though, did it? There's been another attempt. Here in the States."

Weir splayed his fingers over his knees and examined them for a long second before he answered. "Yes. Someone broke into her room and left a tripwire that would have set off a bomb. Lucky for her she's cautious and found it before she set it off."

"Who's your suspect?" Chad cut to the chase.

"The man's name is Frank Harris." Weir pulled out a sheet of paper from his jacket pocket and passed it to Sam, who glanced at it for a moment before handing it to Chad. "According to the investigating officer, Harris has links to a half dozen radical terrorist organizations ranging from Shining Path to Al Qaeda."

All three of them—Sam, Troy and Chad—cursed.

"We can provide a safe location for her to stay—" Sam glanced at Chad, who nodded his agreement, "—complete with armed bodyguards, and a state-of-the-art security system with around the clock coverage. But you're going to have to let us in on the investigation she was running."

"Fair enough." Weir nodded.

Chad left Sam to discuss the monetary details while he considered which safe house to use and who to assign as their principal's guards. He discarded the house in Fredrick as unsuitable. It worked fine for partners seeking distance from a vengeful ex, but with this case, they were talking a more sophisticated threat. The estate in Texas Sam had bought and fitted out the previous year was a possibility, as were the penthouse in New York, the farm just outside Atlanta, or the compound in Vermont. They'd each been set up with a state-of-the-art alarm system, along with a panic room that would be secure even if someone hit it with a hundred pounds of C-4 explosive. For some reason he couldn't name, he ruled out Arlington. New York was out too. It had seen enough terrorism, thanks very much. He checked with the Atlanta office only to discover their safe house was in use. Which left Vermont.

They'd need round-the-clock coverage and someone experienced in dealing with people willing to die to attain their target. He ran through his list of available operatives, weighing each on their merits. The former vice cop Walters? He'd be the best bet as a lead op. The newbie—Campbell—made the list because he hadn't lost that wariness from his hitch in Afghanistan. Wariness was exactly what he wanted, what their client needed. He added and discarded a half-dozen more names. Once he had a plan set in his head, he rejoined the discussion.

Sam leaned back in his chair. "Who are you thinking for lead op?"

Before he could say anything, Troy leaned forward. "Can I recommend Scott Phillips? He's got one of the best strategic minds of anyone at Hauberk."

Phillips? They both knew the operative wasn't one hundred percent recovered from his torture at the hands of the terrorists in Colombia.

"No." Sam's emphatic denial saved Chad from having to denounce Troy's pick. "He can help guard her, but I don't want him as the lead."

“That those people were taken hostage wasn’t his fault, Sam, and you know it. There’s no possible way he could have known they were being set up,” Troy argued, intensity building in his tone. “Plus he’ll be extra cautious *because* of what happened down there. Paranoia can be a good weapon sometimes.”

Sam shook his head. “No. I’ve got a better idea.”

He turned his attention back to Weir. “I’m gonna put Mr. Miller himself here in charge of your lady’s protection, Mr. Weir. He’s former FBI and has learned a few more tricks since we’ve set up Hauberk.”

Damn it. Chad’s irritation increased twelvefold when Weir turned a considering eye on him. “From what I understand he’s been sitting behind a desk for a while. How do I know he’s up to the task?”

“Shee-it.” Sam hissed in a breath. “Who the hell do you think plans and supervises all our ops? The damned janitor?”

The tension in the air thickened when Weir stiffened, making Chad wonder what his story was, and if he was telling them everything about this threat that they needed to know. Finally he nodded. “All right. So, tell me what you’re planning to do to keep her safe.”

“First we’re going to get her out of D.C. We drive her around the city and check for a tail. Then we take her to Dulles and fly her to one of the busier airports—”

“Atlanta or O’Hare,” Troy injected.

“—have her change planes to one of our private jets, changing planes at least twice more.”

“We make it effin’ hard for anyone to follow her path.”

Chad ignored Troy’s interruptions. “Then we stash her in one of our safe houses we have scattered around the country, surround her with a dozen or more heavily armed agents, and keep her safe until the threat can be neutralized."

"Where?"

Weir's condescending smile rankled. Who did he think he was dealing with here? A fucking amateur? "With all due respect, Mr. Weir, if I tell you where she's staying, next thing we know there's a leak somewhere—an email that's compromised, a phone conversation that's overheard and your lady is lying on a slab in the morgue beside a handful of our agents. If you hire us, you'll just have to trust us to keep her safe."

"While she's tucked safely away, we set up a team to smoke Harris out," Sam added. "Since I'm going to be around anyway, I'll lead the team myself."

Weir tapped his index finger on his knee for ten seconds before he nodded. He stood and held out his hand, surprisingly to Chad, not to Sam. "All right, you're in. But if you lose her, if you fuck this up and she gets hurt? I'm coming after you."

"I'll keep her safe." Because who knew if Sam would let him come back. Without Hauberk, without a job to lose himself in, what else did he have left?

Chapter Three

Lauren was lost. Neither Ed nor the Hauberk agent whom Ed introduced as Andy Walters would tell her where they were now or where they were heading. Oh, she'd recognized Atlanta's red soil at their first stop, but they'd switched to a ten-seater Lear and from there they'd landed in a series of unrecognizable municipal airports. Each time they'd landed, she'd wondered aloud if Chad would be meeting them there. Each time Ed scratched his fake beard and shrugged while Andy said nothing at all. She'd given up asking three landings ago when they'd switched from the Lear to a Cessna.

She placed her suitcase at her feet and assessed her surroundings as a white panel van approached. The crisp wind cutting through her thin jacket bore no resemblance to the balmy Georgia weather where they'd first changed planes. No mountains in the distance, no skyscrapers. They could be anywhere in middle America. Or Canada for that matter.

After a simple "stay here", Andy walked across the tarmac toward the van.

Two men jumped out the back, both scanning the area for threats while the driver remained with the van. They'd left their jackets unbuttoned despite the chill in the air, prepared to draw their weapons if challenged. Good. Chad would never have hired wannabe rent-a-cops. These guys were probably ex-police, ex-military. Maybe even a couple of former FBI agents, like Chad. And her.

Andy greeted them then climbed into the van. To warn Chad? She'd never met Walters before, so she couldn't be sure if he knew that she'd formerly been Mrs. Miller or not. If he did know, would he warn Chad and give him an opportunity to back out before they could get him safe?

Moments later Andy reappeared, as did another man. Lauren's heart fluttered into a rapid tattoo then plummeted. It wasn't Chad but Troy McPherson. She barely stifled her huff of disappointment. "What's he doing here? Where's Chad?"

"Watson's probably sending Miller on his own series of hops to make sure he's not followed either," Ed guessed. "That way Harris can't simply follow him to find you."

"You're sure Watson bought your cover story?"

"For now. But we both know Hauberk has some fucking impressive contacts within the DSS that even Cooper doesn't have, so they'll find out I'm not who I say I am soon enough. I figure we've got another twelve hours. Maybe more, maybe less."

"We should have come up with a better cover."

"There wasn't time." He ignored her scowl. "Anyway, once they do figure it out, you and Miller will both be somewhere safe. Who I am won't matter after that. Besides, McPherson knows who you are. If you explain to him about Chad being in danger, he'll help."

He'd help keep *Chad* safe. She wasn't as sure she wouldn't find herself thrown to the wolves.

"While they're not looking..." Ed tucked a strand of her hair behind her ear. To anyone watching, it would appear to be a familiar gesture of a friend, perhaps even a lover. With luck they wouldn't see the transponder he'd tucked into her French braid so she could contact him in an emergency. "It's the only way to keep you both safe, Lauren. Cooper said Harris cracked whatever code they had on the psych files. If he could get in there, who knows if he accessed the rest—you know we can't use any of our own resources."

"I know. There are just so many things that can go wrong. On so many levels."

McPherson said something to one of the men before he and Andy headed their way. His scowl deepened with each step. Troy's gaze flickered between her and Ed, then dropped to her suitcase. His eyes narrowed when he realized she was the only one with luggage.

"You?" He faced Weir. "This is *not* a good idea."

Ed pulled out his cell phone. "Shall I phone your boss and tell him you're refusing the assignment?"

"So call him. Tell him." His Irish accent was thick today, where last time they'd spoken she'd not heard a trace. Did he affect it for show or did it only slip out when he was upset? "Sam won't agree to this either. Standard procedure is the lead op, or anyone else on the detail for that matter, has no personal involvement with the subject. She's his ex-wife for Christ's sake."

Ed tucked his cell phone in his pocket, letting Troy get a look at the Sig Sauer under his jacket. He took off his glasses, pulled off his beard. Without the props, the hardness of his personality was reflected in the sharp planes of his face. "You do it our way or...our way. You don't have a choice."

"Yeah. I do. We put Walters in charge of the op the way Chad originally suggested."

"We can't accept that, Troy." Lauren exchanged a look with her partner. They'd worked together long enough that he knew what she intended. After a moment, Weir nodded his agreement. "Whoever is after me may try to get to me through

Chad. That's the reason we manipulated things the way we did today. We had to keep Chad safe as well."

"Chad's an effin' target?" Troy tossed in a few more epithets, though they weren't in any language she understood. "Might have been nice if you'd let me in on that beforehand. Or Sam."

"We were afraid you'd tell Miller."

Lauren jumped in. "If Chad realized he was the target, you know he'd demand to stay in Washington and fight the threat head on. This way we can both keep him safe."

"By putting you both in the same place? Don't you think that's making it a little too easy for Harris? It would be better if you're kept in separate safe houses." He was right of course. She'd made the same point to Cooper.

Ed must have realized she was about to relent. He folded his arms and glared at Troy. "You don't do things the way we ask, we'll take Miller into protective custody and hold him where you can't reach him. We can also arrest you for interfering with government agents. That wouldn't look so good for Hauberk now, would it Mr. *McPherson*?"

He'd do it too. Ed would call in the cavalry, who would hustle Troy away and convince him to play ball—by fair means or foul—but if it came down to it, they couldn't press charges. After all, the Brigade didn't officially exist, according to the government.

Maybe it was the way Ed emphasized his name, telling him they knew he wasn't who he claimed that had Troy giving a short nod.

Troy held out his hand to her, palm up. "Give me your bloody cell phone."

Damn it. It wasn't unexpected; she would have made the same demand. She'd just hoped they'd trust her. Good thing Ed had tucked the back-up device into her hair. "I'll need to stay in contact with Ed. Otherwise, how will I know when the assignment's over?"

"Oh, we'll let you use our phones once we've verified everything. In the meantime, I want to make sure you don't text the location of where I'm about to take you to James Bond here. Or that he won't use the GPS chip to track you." No trace remained of the broad Irish accent he'd used earlier. "Then there's the added bonus that it'll bug the shit out of you."

He gestured to one of his companions and tossed the phone to him before turning back to her, his hand outstretched again. "Now your purse, if you don't mind, Ms. *Patrick*."

She handed it over without a word. Other than her lipstick, and her fake ID there wasn't anything of worth in it. That was a lesson she'd learned long ago.

Instead of him rummaging through it the way she'd expected, he tossed it to the same man who had her phone.

"If this goes wrong, if Chad gets hurt, then I'm taking you out." Aiming his finger as if it were a gun, Troy pointed to them each in turn. "Both of you."

His hand firm on her elbow, Troy marched her to the van where he told her to "assume the position". He did a thorough pat-down, including a sweep with an electronic wand. She held her breath. The Brigade techs had assured them the device didn't transmit any signal while it was turned off. Andy's sweep after they'd met him hadn't picked up the transponder in Ed's pocket. But she wasn't sure if Troy's equipment was the same type or if it was more efficient at sniffing out electronics. To her relief, Troy didn't run the wand over her hair.

Even so she didn't release her breath until he handed the wand back to the other agent and gestured to the van. "Get in."

She climbed in and took a seat on one of the benches lining

the side. Troy jumped in and sat across from her, his expression hard. "Lauren Miller—excuse me, Ms. *Patrick*—" he gestured to the young agent beside him, "—meet Kris Campbell. He and Walters will be part of your primary team." He narrowed his eyes. "I was supposed to leave you here, but I'm thinking I'll stick around a while."

The unspoken "To make sure you don't fuck up" hung heavy in the air.

The third man, the one who had taken her cell phone and purse, closed the back door from outside. He tapped it twice and the driver set the van in motion.

"Isn't he coming with us?"

"Nope. He's taking your stuff on a little ride all their own. Just to make sure there's no hidden tracking devices in them." Troy glanced out the side of his eyes at her. "You'll get your purse back whenever the hell this assignment's done."

They drove for several hours before stopping at yet another municipal airport. In the cover of a private hanger, Troy loaded her onto a Sikorsky S-76 helicopter where a second pair of agents waited. One she didn't recognize, though she guessed from his posture he was either a cop or military. The second she did recognize though: Scott Phillips, the single hostage who had managed to escape the guerillas in Colombia before the Brigade had rescued the remainder. Scott gave her a cool look before turning his attention to pulling out a well-worn paperback. She might have thought him engrossed if she hadn't realized he'd turned the page only twice in the next hour.

From the buffeting that had her clutching the armrests, she guessed they were flying over mountains but were they the Guadalupes of Texas, or had they'd flown north and were over the foothills of North Dakota's Black Mountains? Then again, thanks to the nap she'd taken who knows how many hours ago, perhaps they'd doubled back and they were over the Appalachians or even the Laurentians.

At the same time she was thinking of their flight into the terrorists' camp in Colombia, the young agent to her left cursed under his breath about it being Afghanistan all over again. Guess it didn't matter what country or what battle, bad weather and bad flights were universal.

She craned her neck to see out the windows and realized twilight had long since come and gone, and all she could see below them was inky blackness.

Scott peered down at the circle of lights that suddenly blazed beneath them and exhaled. "Thank God."

"Please tell me this is our last stop." She covered her mouth and yawned in an effort to pop the pressure building in her ears from the change in altitude.

"What? Are you bored with our company already?" Troy grabbed a strap over the door when a gust of wind caught the helicopter and it swung around. "You're welcome to leave any time you want. No skin off my nose."

Was Troy still pissed off they hadn't tipped him off to their plans earlier? Or maybe he was offended on Chad's behalf? If that was his reasoning, she had no argument. She stared out the window, watching the stars disappear behind the treetops that whipped around in the downdraft of the helicopter's blades. At least Chad had friends who'd stayed with him this time.

As soon as they'd touched down, the lights shut off, leaving them in the dark. "What's stopping anyone else" —an attacker— "from landing their own helicopter?"

"Oh, I think we'd find a way to discourage any unwanted visitors."

"Let me guess, you've armed your guards with surface-to-air missiles."

A dark smile quirked the ends of his lips but he didn't say anything. Holy hell, how had Hauberk managed to acquire SAMs legally? Just who had Sam Watson fucked to get that type of power?

What was she thinking? He probably obtained them from the same place as the Brigade. Cooper Davis had drawn Sam into his circle without Sam even suspecting what was going on. Or did Sam know about Cooper's real identity?

That single connection between Sam and the Brigade's leader sent another frisson of worry through her. There were too many threads hanging on this case, too many possibilities for Harris to infiltrate Hauberk's network.

A camouflaged guard, complete with infra-red goggles and an MP5 machine gun slung over his shoulder, slid open the helicopter door and glanced around the interior. As soon as he recognized Troy, he touched his hand to his forehead as if he were in the military. "Good evening, sir. Everything's secure."

Troy jumped out first then reached up to help her out, his expression grim. "I hope you bloody well know what you're doing."

So did she.

She ducked her head as she jumped to the ground beside him. Instead of the pavement she expected, soft grass cushioned her landing. Crickets chirped as she took a deep breath, hoping to get some sense of where they were. The scent of fresh mown grass and damp earth filled her lungs. No distant roar of a highway, no bright lights indicative of a nearby city bouncing off the few clouds. With only the stars sparkling above and no moon, she couldn't see much beyond the field they were in. Rolling hills silhouetted the horizon, increasing her suspicion they'd gone in a circle and were now back east.

Vermont's Green Mountains? The Appalachians? But where? Tennessee? Pennsylvania? North Carolina? Did it matter? Not as long as Harris couldn't find them.

Her confidence in their plan faltered when she saw Chad at the far edge of the meadow, four men armed with an assortment of MP5s and M4 carbines flanking him. Even with the distance between them, power emanated from him. His alert posture combined with a quiet confidence radiated his awareness of everything surrounding them. No doubt he'd already evaluated everything either as a threat or for use as a possible defense. Would he head straight for the front gate once he found out she was his principal?

His gaze skimmed over her as they approached, then flicked to assess the two agents at her side. Though his expression was bland, there was no mistaking the tension in his shoulders.

She arrived beside Troy just in time to hear him say, "This wasn't my effin' idea."

Chad looked directly at Lauren but she couldn't read his expression; he'd donned the damned implacable mask he'd learned to use thanks to the FBI and the media. "Noted."

Troy glanced over his shoulder and shook his head. "I think I'll hang around a couple days in case you want someone else to take over."

The agents hung back as Chad stuck his hands in his pockets, something he only did if he was nervous. Which meant his pockets were rarely used. "Hello, Lauren."

I'm sorry, please forgive me for leaving you. For not coming back. I despise your sister for what she did to us. I hate myself for trusting her. I've never stopped loving you. I've missed holding you and being held. I've even missed the way you hog the covers at night. "Hello, Chad."

"Let's go inside." Not cold. Not warm either. Business-like. Detached. Like she was a stranger.

Maybe she was.

As they walked toward the waiting Humvee, his palm touched the small of her back, igniting a memory of the first time they'd met at the bar where she'd worked her last year of college. How he'd been so careful with her, so tender and gentle. Oh, he had strength. He'd proven that the way he'd handled the drunken patron who had accosted her. He'd waited around until the end of her shift, his friends having ditched him hours before. Once she was done, he'd escorted her to her car, placing the flat of his hand on her back just the way it was now. The same spark of electricity had zinged through her then too.

Lauren closed her eyes, fighting the guilt welling inside. When she told him what she'd done, when she finally confessed her secret, he'd leave. Worse, he might hate her.

Chapter Four

Chad stared out the Humvee's window in a futile effort to pretend Lauren wasn't sitting mere feet away from him. Did Sam know it was Lauren he'd be protecting?

Damn it, was this all a setup? Some twisted scheme to get them back together? Was Thalia playing one of her manipulative games? Or Sam? No, neither of them liked Lauren. Oh, they'd both liked her well enough until she'd walked away from their marriage. Thalia had been livid on his behalf, while Sam...well, Sam had set him up with an endless number of women. All of whom he'd turned down. Almost all, he corrected himself. It had been almost ten years, and he doubted Lauren had been celibate either. The idea of her being with another man turned his stomach. His gaze slid sideways and he checked her left hand. After all these years why should he feel such satisfaction in not finding a ring? He should want her to be happy. Even if it wasn't with him, damn it.

Something about the whole assignment, about the way Weir had come to them and then the way Sam had suggested he get out from behind the desk and take the assignment had the hairs on the back of his neck standing at a ninety-degree angle. Weir had to have known he worked for Hauberk, had to have known he'd once been married to Lauren. So why seek him out? He ran through the meeting and realized that he'd been manipulated—and from the looks of it, Sam had been part of the manipulation. Which made no sense if Sam knew Lauren would be their principal; there was no way in hell he would have put Chad in charge of her protection. Sam, more than anyone, would realize his objectivity would be skewed. It must be obvious from the way he couldn't stop staring at her ankles, remembering them wrapping about him as he positioned himself at her entrance, that he was anything but objective. His cock stiffened at the memory of the heat of her pussy as he slid deep inside her. Shit yeah, his objectivity was completely shot to hell.

When the Humvee pulled into the garage, he got his first good look at her in the light. There were a few more lines on her face than there had been, no surprise, though fewer than on his. Her hair was longer than it had been last time he'd seen her. Damn it, why was he so turned on by the thought of threading his fingers through her hair, holding her in place while she...Fuck. Fuck. Fuck. *Focus on the mission, not on her sucking your dick, you fucking idiot*!

So much for maintaining any sort of balance. Thank God Troy had said he'd hang around a few days.

Chad led her through the kitchen, introducing her to the couple who took care of the place throughout the year. He'd been here before, for visits and training exercises, so he stood back and watched her. Despite the circles under her eyes, she took the time to greet each of the agents who would be guarding her.

Damn, she looked sexy in that totally oblivious I'm-all-business manner. No one else knew the body hidden beneath that demure white cotton blouse and navy blue slacks. No one else knew the passion and the heat waiting to be released when Lauren let go of her inhibitions. No one else *here* would know, he corrected himself.

As he stood back waiting, he caught Walters slanting him a glance from time to time. Did Andy know Lauren was his ex-wife and now wondered why he hadn't removed himself as lead op? Some great example he was setting to his agents, wasn't he?

Or was Andy attracted to her and wondered if Chad might be jealous if he put a move on her? The little green-eyed monster he thought he'd conquered long ago flared into a dragon that filled the room.

After shooting Andy a narrow glance, Chad grasped Lauren's elbow. "You must be tired. Let me show you your room."

The second he touched her again his whole body reacted as if he'd grabbed a thousand-volt electrical wire—the same sensation he'd had that first night he'd escorted her at the bar. The same way it had each time he'd touched her every day they were married.

"There's an indoor pool, a work-out room, all the comforts of your standard mansion." He'd originally planned to show her them all tonight, but damn it all, he needed distance between them or she'd find herself plastered against the wall, her slacks on the floor at her ankles, her pussy glistening as he buried his cock deep within her.

He pushed open the door to the main bedroom and stood aside, letting her enter first. "I'll show you the rest of the place in the morning."

"No debriefing? Isn't that Hauberk standard operating procedure?"

From the circles beneath her eyes and the heaviness of her lids, she was about to drop. He could have her horizontal in three seconds flat but she wouldn't sleep until he was finished. *Damn it! Focus!* "Sam's got a team working on it. We're safe enough for tonight that we can wait another few hours before we start down that path."

If he had his way, he'd continue the investigation. Until she told him where she'd gone after she'd dropped from his information nets keeping track of her six years ago. Until she told him why she'd done what she'd done years before. Said what she'd said. And not said what he'd needed her to say. *I love you,* like he'd said to her picture a thousand times that first day and the following weeks, followed by *why?*

The pain from coming home that afternoon to discover she'd moved out washed over him. Not in the tidal wave that had once engulfed him. No, time had changed the grief and heartbreak into an acid wash that corroded his honor, his dignity. Having her standing here, so close, captive to his questioning challenged his control.

If he gave into that need, the desire to break her down, he'd never be able to face himself in a mirror again. Those tactics were for the other side.

The bed looming too large in his imagination, he stayed in the middle of the room and let her explore for herself. She opened the closets, frowning as she examined the various track suits, T-shirts and khakis.

Her frown deepened as she fingered a black leather quilted vest. "This is all bullet proof, isn't it?"

"Yes." They'd protect her from close arm fire. Or a sniper. As long as it wasn't a head shot. "For the duration of your stay here, those are the only clothes you'll wear."

"They must have cost Sam a small fortune."

He forced his jaw to unlock. Obviously time hadn't softened her opinion of Sam. "Don't worry about that. Hauberk's doing quite well, in case you haven't heard."

After releasing a slow breath, Lauren nodded. "I wasn't

trying to be argumentative. I'm proud of what you've build Hauberk up to be. I'm glad you found somewhere to keep you challenged."

Not enough to come back to him. Or even pick up the phone and call him.

She carefully closed the closet door and walked to the window. Probably trying to figure out where she was, he'd wager. In the morning, she may figure out which state they were in. It didn't matter if she knew where they were or not. What mattered was that no one else discovered their location.

"Did you mean what you said to Troy?" she asked after a long moment had passed. "About blaming yourself if anything happened to me?"

"Yes." *I worry about everything when it comes to you.*

He shut the drape she'd opened, aware he was closing them in completely from prying eyes, aware of the closed door to the hall, how she stood less than a foot away from him, and the massive bed behind her. The subtle fragrance of her perfume tickled his nose. It was the perfume he'd bought her for her birthday the first year they'd been together.

The dark urges, the ones he'd denied for so long, reared up, sending a finger of flame down his spine. His cock hardened, and his balls drew close to his body as his imagination exploded. He wanted to strip her naked and tie her to the bed, leaving her spread eagled and vulnerable. He'd reclaim every inch of her, make a meal of her before spreading her thighs and reminding her who had made her come. Then he'd flip her onto her stomach and take her anally too. And when they were all done, she'd admit she'd never had another lover satisfy her like he could.

What if she had?

Maybe Lauren sensed his thoughts; more likely she'd

noticed his burgeoning hard-on, because she stepped away from him. "Are you worried someone might be watching us with a high-powered scope?"

In truth, he wasn't worried about a sniper. She couldn't see how the lights penetrated her linen skirt, how they outlined her trim legs and the V they formed. That the men patrolling the grounds might see her silhouette and have their own fantasies annoyed him no end. "The windows are certified bulletproof, but I'd prefer not to give them a target."

Goddamn it, how many times did they lecture the newbies about maintaining distance and yet here he was, the "I want to fuck you, who cares about anything out there that might put you in danger" poster child.

"Guess that means my five-mile run is off the agenda in the morning?"

His brain dredged up a memory of one of their jogs during their honeymoon. Halfway through their run, Lauren had pointed out a field filled with clover and daisies, bees lazily buzzing from blossom to blossom around them. He'd dragged her into the thigh-high grasses, the thickness of the clover hiding them as he'd undressed her, made love to her. The field echoed with her laughter when he'd plucked a daisy and tickled her with it. Her smile had been brighter than the sun, the sheen of sweat glistening on her skin after he'd rolled off her still made his heart quicken. Finding a field was out of the question, but there was a gazebo overlooking the pond in the valley. If he remembered correctly there was a sofa bed that would cushion them nicely.

Why did he keep imagining them together again? She'd divorced him. Moved out. Moved on.

He stomped the fantasy of them getting back together, even for the night, under his heel. "There's a treadmill in the weight room you can use."

She stopped at the side of the bed, her fingers trailing over the hand-made quilt. She could probably tell him what type it was—the styles all had names like wedding ring or log cabin, but damned if he could tell one from the other. All that mattered to him was that it would keep her warm. Pity no one made the damned things with a layer of Kevlar. Maybe then he'd sleep easier.

"Where are you sleeping?"

Part of him wanted to answer "I'm sleeping in that bed right beside you, just like your husband should," but that part of their marriage had ended even before she'd walked out the door. He shoved his emotions aside. If she wanted a business-like relationship, that's what he'd give her. Tonight. After that the gloves came off.

He stalked to the connecting door and wrenched it open. "I'll be in here. The rest of the team are scattered about the various floors."

Her expression didn't change, her shoulders didn't relax. Did she wish he were sleeping on a different floor? Maybe he should change rooms with Andy or Troy. Distance between them might make this assignment more bearable.

"There are snipers with infrared goggles on the roof, a small platoon of armed guards patrolling the perimeter of the estate, along with a dozen attack dogs protecting the grounds." He kept his voice even, flat. Unemotional. The complete opposite of the needs clawing his guts. "The house has the latest in security—infrared and motion detectors. The doors and windows are wired, and of course you've noticed the cameras in all the main areas. If you want to leave the room tonight, come get me first and I'll give the detail a heads-up that you're on the move." And accompany her anywhere she went.

"Afraid I might be mistaken for an intruder?" From the amusement in her voice, she wasn't taking this threat seriously. Damn it. She'd know that despite the precautions they'd taken, there was always a possibility their security could be breached.

"Let me know if you leave the room." He pointed to the button on the side of the night table. "Until we get you set up with a personal panic button, press this to summon the troops if there's any trouble. There's another one in the bathroom, as well as in the closet. Any one of them will set off the alarm and bring the whole team running."

She nodded her head in approval. Her fingers stroked the damned quilt, though he wondered if she was aware of what she was doing.

"Turn this and it'll give you access to your panic room." He turned the center of a rose carved into the mantel. A panel beside the fireplace sprang open revealing a small dark area no bigger than the closet.

She walked closer to examine the tiny room. "Is that a fireman's pole?"

He nodded, unable to stop focusing on how her lips were parted in amusement, soft and plump, glistening with traces of her lip gloss. Kissable.

Focus on the mission, not your goddamned dick. Damn it, she was his principal. She was in danger and needed him focused on her protection.

Why the hell had he let Sam talk him into accepting this assignment? He should leave, let Troy take over the job; he was staying anyway. Except he couldn't walk away. Not now. Not when there was a chance she might finally answer his questions.

He struggled to keep his tone even. "It leads to a room in the basement. It has its own air supply, first aid supplies, encrypted radio to head office, a direct line to the local police, as well as enough food and water for a month."

"Sounds more like a bomb shelter."

"It's that as well. There's a twenty-foot drop straight down, so make sure you've got a good grasp on the pole before you step off. Tomorrow we'll do a practice run."

Chapter Five

He was so cold, so controlled. The struggle to keep her disappointment from showing challenged Lauren. Did he not feel anything for her anymore? Did he have none of the desire, none of the need that had tied them together? The desire that had flared inside her, setting her body aglow as soon as she'd seen him? The need for him hadn't lessened over the years. If anything, he was more attractive than he'd been before. She'd always found a man with just a hint of silver at his temples sexy.

How could she get him to stay? To listen to her with an open mind?

She took a step closer. *Please don't let him leave. Don't let him close the door between our rooms and shut me out completely.*

She toyed with the buttons of her blouse. She'd left the top two undone out of habit, but now she toyed with the next one, undoing it, then the next. The fabric parted just enough to show the lace of her chemise. He'd always preferred the fantasy of wondering what was beneath, letting his imagination take over. "Thank you for volunteering to guard me. I was surprised when they said you'd be the lead op."

She *had* been surprised, she realized. She'd been half expecting them to call the whole thing off. Fear that she'd screw things up even more and lose any chance for a reconciliation set in, leaving her frozen deep into her bones.

"I should go." His voice was rough but at least he hadn't moved.

"Please don't." She touched his forearm, letting her fingers rest on him. Heat rose through his cotton shirt, warming her. He was leaner than he'd been. Different. Yet the same. "I don't think I could get to sleep, not after that helicopter ride."

His gaze dropped to her fingers, a frown creasing his forehead. "I'd forgotten you don't like riding in helicopters. Was the flight bad?"

"It could have been better." *You could have been with me.* "There was a bit of turbulence coming over the hills." Or were they mountains? She still hadn't decided. "I haven't had much to eat. Maybe we could find the kitchen, rustle up a sandwich. Talk." About so many things she didn't know where to start. An explanation for why she'd left? For not contacting him? Or even where she'd been and what she'd been doing? Except neither of those were possible thanks to the Brigade's rigid secrecy agreement.

"I'll call the kitchen and ask if they can bring something up for you. As for talking..." He scrubbed his face with his hands, breaking her contact with him. "We can talk tomorrow when we're both fresh." He made touching him impossible by walking to the door and standing inside his room. "When we've both had a chance to sleep on things."

"Stay. I don't want to be alone tonight." Like she'd been for so long.

If she'd had any question he could still love her, the look he gave her removed any doubt. There was no trace of the predator on the hunt he'd had when they were first dating or even five minutes ago, the dominant man determined to win her. This look spoke of the depth of his love and longing. His voice, though controlled, revealed his pain and need even though it was barely above a whisper, husky as if he'd been screaming all night. "I don't think that's a good idea."

"I do." She walked toward him, trying to be quiet, desperate not to give in to the urge to fall at his feet and prove herself to him. If she did, he might react like a wounded animal. One that could turn on her and rip her limb from limb.

No doubts tonight, she told herself, afraid to speak out loud, afraid of breaking whatever force was holding them together. She undid the remaining buttons, tugged her blouse from her slacks and let it drop from her shoulders onto the floor.

His gaze dropped to the lace of her chemise where her nipples had hardened. He'd always loved her breasts, loved touching them, cupping them, kissing them. She debated pulling the chemise over her head, letting him view them unencumbered but decided the peep show might be more provocative. It felt strange to be deliberately leading him on, to have to seduce him. She shimmied out of her slacks and stepped out of them, leaving them in a heap on the floor beside her blouse. Seconds later, her thong rested on top of the pile.

One moment he was clutching the door frame, the next moment she was flattened against it, his thigh between her legs, holding her in place. His voice rasped as he asked, "What's your game, Lauren?"

"I'm not playing a game, Chad." *Just doing a lousy job of seducing you.*

He closed his eyes for just a second before meeting her gaze again. "So it's just sex you're looking for? You want to fuck and that's it? Like an itch you want to scratch?"

We cared more about fucking than making sure Emily didn't die, a tiny voice in the back of her head nagged. A voice she thought she'd long since banished. "I miss you. I miss us."

His lips hovered centimeters above hers, his breath warm on her cheek, his eyes locked on her mouth. She expected him to lean down, to take charge, to kiss her. But he didn't. Instead he held himself in check with a rigid control, as if he were fighting a battle. And winning.

"I don't want just one night, Lauren. I want it all back again—us, the way we were. We both know that's not going to happen."

All her doubts crumbled into dust. He wanted her still. "We don't know that."

She tilted her chin and closed the distance between them until her lips brushed his. He didn't move, letting her tongue slide against the seam joining them but not allowing her entry. She wouldn't beg but if he wouldn't accept her kiss, she'd find another way past his defenses.

Her hands flattened over his chest, seeking his shirt buttons. He didn't move as she undid them one by one. His stomach muscles tensed when she parted the opening of his shirt and touched bare skin. She affected him, no matter how hard he tried to hide it. She was so close. If she could just convince him to let go, to give her a chance...she traced the curve of his stomach, up to his pectorals. *Love me. Please.*

As if she'd touched a switch, his body shuddered beneath her fingers. He drew a deep breath, then his lips captured hers, taking command of the kiss. His tongue swept over her lips as if he were sampling her, preparing to feast upon her. He adjusted the angle of his head; his chin rasped over hers, the heat of the razor burn rousing a lingering reminder of their lovemaking long ago.

This was what she'd remembered, what she'd dreamed of all these years. Wanted. Needed.

Yet he hadn't touched her with anything but his mouth. She wanted his hands on her, all over her, every inch of his body touching hers. His chest, his stomach, his hips. More than the hard length of his thigh holding her in place.

Her hands slid around his waist in an attempt to pull him closer but he resisted her attempts. Damn it, if he wouldn't come to her, she'd go to him.

She shifted until they were chest to chest, cradling his erection against her mound, relieved to feel the proof that he wanted her as much as she needed him. The pressure against her chest increased when he captured her wrists, dragged them over her head. *God yes, like that. Take me hard and fast, the way I love.*

Their combined breathing was heavy and harsh in the room as they stood there, panting. Waiting. The hell with waiting. She'd waited too long for this chance, she wasn't going to let it slip away. Holding her breath, she ground her hips against his erection.

With a groan she felt to her toes, Chad dropped his head to her shoulder. His mouth sought out the spot beneath her ear, a spot he'd long ago learned connected straight to her pussy. His teeth nipped the spot, his tongue soothed the sting. Pain followed by pleasure. He repeated it. So hard and fast was out. Slow and easy was nice too.

Without warning, he straightened, releasing her. Instead of backing away, his fingers combed through her hair, one hand cupping the back of her head, holding her in place. "Tell me you don't want this."

"I can't. I *do* want this."

I want to go to bed with you lying beside me, knowing you'll be there in the morning. I want to make you understand why I had to leave, take the pain away that I caused you. I want us. The way we once were. Before.

Before the photographers invaded their privacy. Before Emily's death. If it hadn't been for his hold on her, she would have swayed. Instead, she forced the guilt, the grief, back into their cubbyhole and slammed the door she'd created to hold them back.

With a gentle pressure, he pushed her to her knees.

"You know what I want." His voice was rough, as if he'd been shouting in a smoke-filled room all night. Did he realize he only sounded like that when she was in front of him like this? She clung to the knowledge that she still had the power to excite him.

Her fingers shook as she reached for his fly, though with excitement or fear that he'd stop her she wasn't sure.

Could he feel how the blood raced through her veins? Or hear her heart pounding like a bass drum with each inch his zipper lowered? Her breath escaped in a soft puff as she released his erection from its tight confines. She leaned her forehead against his belly, loving the feel of the crisp mat of hair that tickled her nose, the strength of the warm shaft against her cheek. This was where she'd wanted to be for years but never believed she'd experience again. To touch him, to smell him and taste him.

Cupping his behind, she pulled back and nuzzled his cock. Her mouth watering in anticipation, she ran her tongue over the heavy crown. He moaned and his fingers tightened in her hair when she took his whole shaft in her mouth, her lips closing round him adding extra pressure. The globes of his ass tightened as he rocked into her in a slow, steady rhythm. Her body heated at the familiarity of the act. The memories of his taste, his scent, escalated her need for release. She moaned, dropping one hand from his ass to finger her clit.

Whether it was the moan or the loss of contact, he tightened his grip on her hair and pulled her off. “Stop.”

He hauled her to her feet, sliding one arm beneath her knee. He kissed her—there was nothing gentle about it. It was hard, demanding. The way she loved. His tongue thrust into her mouth, claiming every inch of her. He broke it off, moving instead to the side of her neck, finding the spot that had her sucking in her breath. She dropped her own mouth to the tender spot where his neck met his shoulder, nipping with her teeth, sucking, leaving her own mark on him, somewhere that would be hidden by his collar. Somewhere no one else would see, but she’d know it was there.

The smooth head of his cock slid between her folds. It brushed over her clit, and withdrew, teasing her until her toes curled against the floor and she couldn’t take it anymore. She slipped a hand between them and guided his cock to her entrance.

With a ferocity he’d never shown before, he thrust deep then stayed motionless until his body vibrated with the need to continue. “Do you want this?”

She tilted her hips, closing her eyes at the delicious friction of him filling her. She loved it when he let his aggressive side loose, commanding. Powerful. God, she’d missed this. Missed him. “I want you. I’ve only ever wanted you, Chad.”

His whole body stiffened, the only warning before he withdrew from her. “Bullshit. You divorced me, remember?”

With a cry, she reached out to catch him when he lifted his pants and refastened his fly. He snatched up her shirt and threw it at her. “You even changed your goddamned name back to Patrick as soon as the divorce went through.”

She straightened her shoulders. He deserved the truth. “I couldn’t stay with you—”

"You were very clear about that. You couldn't be associated with me. What woman wants a man who is more concerned with his sister's life than his wife's career?"

Is that what he thought? Had she really given him that impression? No, more likely Thalia had. "That's not why I left."

"Maybe that wasn't the final straw that drove you out, but it was a big part of it, wasn't it? You never understood why I went against orders, did you?"

"I understood. I still don't agree with your decision to send people in undercover, though I understood why you did it." She deliberately didn't name Sam. "But that's not why I went to England."

"It doesn't matter anymore. Our marriage is over. You got what you wanted. You don't get what you want this time." He released her and opened the door between their rooms. He stopped on the threshold and spoke over his shoulder. "I'll make sure you're protected from this Harris asshole. But once he's neutralized? I don't want to see you again."

Once the door closed behind him, Lauren walked up to it, pressed her forehead against the cool panel and whispered, "I'm not going let you walk away until you've listened to me. Until you believe I left you because I loved you. Not because I didn't."

Chapter Six

Chad rested against the closed door, stifling an urge to bang his head against it. What the hell had he just done? How had he let it get that far?

I've only ever wanted you. Bull. Shit.

Not after the way she'd had the divorce papers delivered to him. In front of the press by a goddamned process server who looked like he should still be in junior high and hadn't even started shaving yet. The kid was intimidated about serving a guy wearing a gun and had stuttered when he'd asked Chad his name. At least until he spotted the cameras. Then he'd adopted a swagger worthy of a rap star.

At least Sam had his back. Once they had Hauberk up and running, Sam had taken on that damned firm in a long bloody takeover. Hauberk had gained a lot of new customers when they'd finally emerged victorious and that had set them on the path to where they were now—the biggest, most reputable personal protection firm on the east coast.

He stomped into the bathroom and turned on the shower. He undid his shirt buttons, barely stopping himself from ripping the damned shirt off. His still-rampant hard-on caused him some grief with the zipper, but soon his trousers sailed across the bathroom to land in a heap in the corner. Goddamn her.

I'm not playing a game.

Damned straight she was playing a game. With his nuts as the dice.

He stepped into the shower, not caring that the water was too hot. Served him right. He grabbed a bar of soap and lathered his hands. Why the hell had he stopped? Why hadn't he taken his due?

Because he'd be damned if he'd let her drag him back into the hell of thinking she cared for him.

His soapy fist wrapped around his cock, jerking it rapidly. He should have taken his time with her. Tied her to the bed. Teased her to the point of orgasm then left her wanting the way she'd done with him. Or taken her hard, worrying only about pleasing himself.

Fuck. He'd forgotten to use a condom. Who knew who she'd been with? How could he have been so fucking stupid? Because he'd let himself forget they weren't married, forgotten that their rules for sex had changed with the stroke of a judge's pen.

He'd walked on eggshells for too damned long around her. Let her turn away from him when they were in bed for almost a year. Only to come home and find she'd moved out, run all the way to fucking England. He fisted his dick with hard, angry strokes. So he'd made a decision at work without consulting her. That was his fucking job. To make decisions. Didn't she understand he'd had no choice but to send Sam and Jill in undercover? That no one else was stepping up to the plate to protect Thalia? That it was his duty to protect his sister? The same as it was to protect Lauren? The way he'd failed to protect Emily.

With a roar, he slammed his fist into the wall, not caring that the tile cracked. Oh, God, Emily. Even after the coroner's report proved there was nothing they could have done, Lauren had blamed him for Em's death. Hell, how could he blame her? He blamed himself. There had to have been something he could have done but Emily had been cold and rigid even before he'd tried CPR. He slumped against the wall, letting the water cascade over him. Maybe if they had gotten up earlier instead of sleeping in that morning, maybe if...like it had every other time he tried to think of something he could have done, he came up blank.

Enough of this shit, he finally told himself.

After roughly applying the soap to the rest of his body, he ducked his head under the shower then shut off the water. He grabbed a towel as he considered the question of what he needed to do now.

Phone Sam. Find out if he knew that Lauren would be his principal.

Probably not, he decided. If he had, Sam would have moved heaven and earth to make sure Chad had *not* been assigned as her lead op; Sam didn't like Lauren any more than she liked him.

So Sam had been manipulated too. No easy feat.

He tossed the towel over the shower rail and ensured the edges were aligned before picking up his clothes where he'd dropped them. Once they were properly folded, he strode naked into his room.

Maybe Weir had access to one of Sam's contacts? Sam's little birdie, the one who put the bug in his ear about the upcoming article?

He stopped in the middle of the room. That's where he had to look. Would Sam tell him who had given him the scoop? Once he found out that he'd been manipulated, damned straight he would. Sam would be as pissed as he was right now. Then Sam would ensure that birdie would sing soprano for the rest of his fucking life. He grabbed a shirt out of the closet and replaced the hanger. The routine of dressing, doing up each button one by one helped him focus. His shirt properly buttoned, he grabbed a pair of underwear from the dresser, smoothing the pile he'd disturbed. A clean pair of freshly pressed dress pants were shaken out, and jerked on. Socks. Black. Calf-length so no ankle showed.

By the time he was completely dressed, his movements were smooth, his thoughts focused. Only then did he pick up his BlackBerry and punch in Sam's number.

No answer.

After leaving a voice message, he booted up his laptop and logged onto Hauberk's VPN.

"*Dear Sam, I respectfully request to be transferred....*" No, that wasn't right. "*Sam, I need a favor...*"

Not once had he asked to be taken off a case. Not with the FBI and not with Hauberk. So, damn it, he wasn't taking no for an answer.

A half hour—and numerous deletions—later he finally hit send.

An hour later, he was checking his email for...well, he'd given up counting how many times he'd hit "check mail", when there was a knock at the hallway door. Before he could respond, it opened and Troy walked in.

"Thought you'd like to know the extra men just arrived." Troy closed the door behind him and rested against it. "I've handed out the rotation you drew up. Everything should be good to go."

"Thanks, but I could have handled it."

"I know but I was there checking out the cameras and everything else, so I took care of it." Instead of leaving the way

Chad had expected, Troy stayed in place. He tilted his head to one side as he considered Chad. "You okay, mate?"

Ah. So that was the purpose of visiting in person. Chad nodded. "I admit I was surprised to see her."

His answer didn't satisfy Troy. "Sorry I couldn't give you any more warning than I did, but—"

So he hadn't known it would be Lauren he was escorting either. "It's okay. You were following protocol. You couldn't call me. I understand."

Troy pushed away from the door and wandered into the room. "Helluva a shock for me too when I recognized her."

He'd recognized her? "How did you know her? You've never met her before."

There was a long pause. When Troy responded he didn't look at Chad, and he kept his voice low. "I know about the picture you keep in your desk." He finally looked up. "I wasn't trying to snoop but you were off somewhere—at some meeting with a client or something and we needed a file. Sandy wasn't there so I went through your desk."

Ah. Here he'd been thinking...who knows what he'd been thinking. "Don't worry about it."

There was another pause. "Are you leaving in the morning?"

In other words, was Troy to take over?

Would Troy keep Lauren safe? Of course. So why the hesitation in telling Troy he'd already asked to be transferred? "It's under consideration. I tried to get a hold of Sam earlier, but I haven't heard back from him yet."

"Maybe he's trying to smooth things over with Rosie for cancelling their vacation."

Which meant they were probably jumping each other's

bones on the desk. Or in that fucking huge shower.

Maybe he was just jealous that Sam's love life had finally come together. Damned stubborn bastard had been closing himself off since Jill's death; it was good to see him finally find someone to love again. Which brought Chad right back around to his original hunch—he'd been set up. Pinching the bridge of his nose, Chad closed his eyes. "Fuck."

He opened his eyes and shot Troy a hard glare. "Is this some way he's come up with to try to force me to get over her? Or get her out of my system or something?"

"Don't know what you're talking about, mate." Troy met his gaze evenly, his voice unaffected. If he'd been anyone else Chad would swear he was telling the truth, but Troy was a consummate liar.

"Why would Weir come to Hauberk if he knew Lauren and I had been married? No one in their right mind would go to an ex-husband to protect a woman." He ran through their conversation again. "No. It's too coincidental."

"And you don't like coincidences." Troy took a deep breath but not once did he break Chad's gaze. "I know you don't believe me right now but swear to God, I had no idea it would be your ex that I'd be escorting." Instead of shutting the fuck up, Troy continued, "You're a better man than me. If it had been my ex, I would have shown her the gate and told her to fend for herself."

He'd considered it. Seriously. Heaven help him if he had to be around her another day. Now he'd had a taste of her, a reminder of what she felt like around him, his dick had taken over his thinking and was seriously planning the various ways he could get her horizontal next time. Not good. "Look, since you're planning on hanging around a couple extra days anyway, why don't I just head back to D.C. now?"

Troy's gaze might have been a laser beam from the look he shot him. "You still fancy her, don't you?"

Fancy her? He'd just jerked off fantasizing about her; that was a big affirmative. "We're divorced."

"That's just a piece of paper, isn't it?" Troy tapped his chest. "But here, inside. That part of you wants another go at her, doesn't it?"

"No."

Annoyed at the line of thought Troy's questions were taking, he stomped into the bathroom and picked up his razor, packing it neatly in its case. When had he decided to leave in the morning whether he'd heard from Sam or not?

"From the looks of your neck, I'd say you may have already had another go at her." Troy had followed him, damn it, and now leaned against the doorframe.

A glance in the mirror revealed Lauren had left a mark on his neck. Damn it, why hadn't he seen that earlier? Because he was too damned busy whacking off. He grabbed the toothpaste and toothbrush and tucked them into their compartment. "Why are you so interested anyway? What the fuck is it to you?"

Troy moved aside when Chad pushed past, trailing him to the bedroom like a goddamned lost puppy. "I may not have been married, but I do know a thing or two about women and how they wind up a man's guts."

Maybe Troy knew about fucking them, but he knew jackshit about keeping them. Then again what did Chad know? He was batting O for one right now, wasn't he? "I'm not about to go crawling back on my hands and knees. She was damned clear she didn't want anything to do with me. She thought..."

Troy waited a long moment before prompting, "What did she think?"

"It doesn't matter."

"It does, though doesn't it? Otherwise you wouldn't have mentioned it."

Unwilling to slog through that emotional swampland, Chad shrugged one shoulder. "She put up with a lot of shit when we were married. Not to mention how the press dragged her through the mud right along with me. Everyone at the bureau thought she'd known what I'd done and had helped cover it up. They made it impossible for her to work there anymore so she ended up having to quit. Even in our personal life—friends she'd had since high school dumped her because of what the press was saying about us."

He'd already lost her by then. She'd pulled away from him after Emily's death. He'd not realized why until that last big fight. By then it had been too late to do anything.

"I'd say they weren't good friends if they walked away when she needed them."

It took Chad a moment to realize what Troy was talking about. "It doesn't matter. Lauren was right. It was my fault the marriage didn't work."

Chad walked to the window and stared out, assessing the guards patrolling the grounds. *What were the guards he couldn't see doing? Were they alert to their surroundings? Or were they goofing off, texting their girlfriends or playing some game they'd downloaded on their cell phone?*

"Do you really believe that? That it was your fault?"

"I'm the one who fucked up. I'm the reason she ended up with her picture splashed over the fucking tabloids." How they'd managed to get that video of the two of them in their bedroom he still hadn't discovered.

"Bugger that," Troy snarled. "Stop feeling so goddamned sorry for yourself, man. From what I've heard, there was nothing you could have done to have saved your daughter's life. People die and most times there's nothing you can do about it but suck it up and move on."

Chad whirled to face him. "You're preaching to the choir about death. I know all about it. My father was killed in the line of duty—shot by a goddamned drug addict during a routine traffic stop. My mother was murdered eight years later." He clenched his fists "Less than a year after Emily died, my sister got shot. She may not be dead but she's in a wheelchair because I couldn't protect her. So do not talk to me about how *people die.*"

"Take your head out of your goddamned arse for once and stop blaming yourself. You were, what, eleven when your father was killed? There is no way you can blame yourself for that. You were living in Boston when that sick bastard lured your mother into showing him that home she had up for sale. There was nothing you could have done to have helped. There was nothing anyone could have done. As for your daughter, her death wasn't your fault either. It is what it is. Stop blaming yourself."

It is what it is. How he hated that phrase. Nothing was as it should be. The anger, the ire, drained from Chad as if Troy had pulled a plug, leaving him with an emptiness that was even worse. "I keep thinking I should have seen something, some sign."

Troy squeezed his shoulder. "Lauren feels the same way. Not about you being responsible, but that she should have seen something too. You two need to talk before you leave, about that if nothing else."

"How would you know?"

"I just do."

They'd been stuck on a plane together for hours with

nothing to do. If Troy had recognized her, maybe they'd talked. He closed the cover on his suitcase and zipped it shut. *Stay. I don't want to be alone tonight.*

What about tomorrow night? Or last night? Or the night before? She'd been the one to run away last time, now he was walking away from her. Self-preservation, instinct, he didn't know which was placing the suitcase by the door, but he'd be damned if he'd let her rip his heart from his chest again.

Maybe that was the question he should be asking himself: why did she still have the power to hurt him after all these years?

"Because you still love her. More's the pity."

He stared at Troy. "What?"

"You asked how she still had the power to hurt you."

He'd said that out loud?

"I know you look at that picture in your desk a half dozen times a day. You still love her." Troy tapped the top of Chad's suitcase. "So, what are you going to do about it? You going to run? Because that hasn't worked for either of you so far, has it?"

Chapter Seven

From the brightness of the clouds overhead, the sun was up on the other side of the mountains, though it had yet to reach the lower edges of the hill. A thick mat of pine needles and already-fallen leaves littered the path, crunching beneath her feet as Lauren jogged along the path. She ducked beneath an overhanging branch, taking care to make sure it didn't fling back into her companion's face.

She'd hoped to slip out of her room that morning without anyone noticing. But as soon as her door had opened, Andy had stepped out. The lack of time between his door opening and hers made her wonder if he'd been listening for her. Then she noticed the camera mounted on the wall opposite her door. Not listening. Watching.

She glanced back to assess him. Like her, he'd dressed for the occasion, although his holster held a Glock whereas hers had a Sig Sauer. Something about the way he carried himself told her he'd not be afraid to use it. An intricate full-arm tattoo flowered from beneath his tee's sleeve, stopping just above the wrist. Probably so it wouldn't show beneath a dress shirt. "How far do you normally run?"

Andy ducked beneath a tree branch before he answered, "About five K. I run more on the weekends."

They'd run the perimeter of the compound—or the estate,

as Chad referred to it—twice, which meant they were approaching the length of a regular run for them both. Although there was a slight sheen of sweat on his forehead, Andy wasn't breathing hard yet, which gave her the impression "more" probably meant he ran marathons. What impressed her most was that they weren't running on a smooth city sidewalk. The rough trail they followed wound its way up and down the side of the...well, it was more than a hill but less than a mountain. They were high enough that the air was thinner than in D.C. Not as thin as in Colombia, but Andy wasn't showing any signs of having trouble getting enough oxygen.

Face it, she told herself, *the man was in shape.* Chad had chosen his people well.

Pounding on the track behind them had her turning and ducking behind the nearest tree. Her hand was still reaching for her holster when she realized Andy already had his gun drawn and his body placed between her and whoever was intent upon catching them. Two seconds later, Troy jogged into sight and Andy lowered his weapon. "Hey, boss, what's up?"

Troy hardly looked at his man as he spoke, his focus completely on Lauren. "I'll take over here. Why don't you get some grub?"

His gun holstered, Andy nodded and sprinted off toward the main house.

Lauren stepped back onto the path, watching him disappear down the hill. "He's good."

"He is. Damned good. But I wasn't the one who hired him initially. That was all your ex-husband's doing." With the emphasis on ex. "Thought you should know—Chad's asked to be reassigned."

Shit. "You can't let him leave. Not if you want him to stay alive."

His hand slapped arrhythmically against his thigh as he stared off in the distance, no doubt considering the same ramifications and alternatives they'd already gone over. "How long do you think you're going to be able to fool him?"

"Hopefully until we catch Harris."

He turned a bland look on her. "That's not what I was referring to."

This was not a conversation she wanted to have. With a sigh, and a silent prayer that Troy wouldn't follow, Lauren reversed her course.

"Running won't help. I want an answer and I want it now."

"I'll answer your question once we're farther away. I don't want Chad overhearing this conversation." She pushed on, speeding up if he got too close. The muscles in Lauren's legs ached, protesting each step she took as the path led back up the side of the hill.

"You're not going to lose me if that's what you're hoping," he said finally, not even breathing heavily, goddamn him. "Now tell me, when are you going to tell him the truth?"

"After we neutralize the threat." Then she'd lock them both in her room until he agreed to give their marriage another chance. Or he'd convinced her there was no way she deserved one. Which was more likely.

He slapped at the branch she'd pushed out of her way but threatened to hit him. "Why don't you just tell him the truth? It's his life—he should get a choice in how it plays out."

"So why didn't you say something to him in the office when the arrangements were being made? You could have told him last night too, but you didn't." If he had, Chad wouldn't be sleeping at the desk in his bedroom the way he had been when she'd checked on him.

Troy cursed again. “Let’s get this straight; I’m not doing this for you. I’m doing it for him. Poor bugger’s been through enough without Cooper and you playing mind games on him. He’s had enough of that, don’t you think?”

She’d had enough mind games to last her a lifetime. Thalia’s. Cooper’s. Was that what she was doing to Chad? Manipulating him? No. Other than keeping him safe, once Harris was found, she’d accept whatever decision he made. For better or worse. She ducked under an overhanging branch. “It’s not a game.”

He grabbed her and forced her to face him. “You know what I don’t get? You work for an organization that’s sanctioned both by the feds and the U.N. for all you try to claim it’s not associated with any of them. Which means you probably have a safe house or two of your own hidden away. Why not just grab Chad and protect him yourselves?”

“That’s not our style.”

“Bullshit.” His gaze hardened. “You’ve been infiltrated, haven’t you? Harris is one of your guys, isn’t he?”

She turned her back on Troy and started running again. If he wanted to continue the conversation, he’d have to follow her. Which the bastard did, damn it.

“What? Didn’t like being questioned? Fine, you’ll have to answer Chad’s questions later.”

“I know.” God help her then.

“Here’s another question for you: why did you do this? Arrange to be placed in the same facility as him? Weir’s story could have served its purpose—we could have guarded you separate from him. But you guys manipulated us just so you two would be put together. Why is that?”

“It’s none of your business.”

"Yeah, lady, it is. Miller is my friend and I don't like people who playing fucking mind games with my friends."

"Guess what, you don't know everything about me. Or Chad. Or our marriage."

"I know more than you think."

"You know nothing but what you overheard when I was talking with Thalia." Half the building had heard that argument.

"I know you ran away after accusing him publicly of having been responsible for the death of your daughter."

She stumbled and had to grab onto a sapling to steady herself. "You don't know what you're talking about. You weren't there."

"No, I wasn't there but I know what you left behind. Chad's a man with more dignity and honor than most men have these days. A man who was only trying to protect his family the best way he knew how, and you walked away from him when he needed you."

"I was there for him while the press camped on our front lawn, taking pictures through the cracks in the blinds that got plastered over the internet for anyone and their brother to see. I lived with the headlines speculating if we were into sex games like those from Thalia's club. Do you have any idea what it's like to be the butt of night show monologue jokes when a video of you and your husband having sex goes viral?" She still hadn't figured out how they'd filmed that footage. "I lived with the neighbors who gave us sideways glances every time we left our front door, with those who didn't bother with glances but with outright suggestions of what they wanted me to do for them. You weren't there when I discovered my co-workers were passing around Photoshopped pictures of me or hear the snickers and suggestions when I walked past them."

She whirled away from him and stared at the trees swaying

overhead. Her body quivered, torn between wanting to race along the path, to put as much space between her and Troy as she could, and decking the smug bastard. "You weren't there when the press followed us to the cemetery to visit Emily's grave on her first birthday." What should have been her first birthday.

"Do you know how it felt to have to watch the news showing your daughter's gravesite being trampled by press who didn't give a damn about respect? To find graffiti and damage done to her gravestone the next day?" She forced herself to face him again. "I had to deal with the catcalls and hate mail accusing us of being single-handedly responsible for 9/11. I was there for the death threats. And the bomb threats. Me. Not you. So don't you dare judge me."

"No, I wasn't there." His voice was soft, almost gentle, but the intensity in his gaze, his white-knuckled fists, told her he was barely hanging on to his own temper. "But Chad was. And you let him think it was all his fault when it wasn't."

"I didn't." She closed her eyes and swayed. She had. Which was one of the reasons she was here, wasn't it?

"I know what you told him, Lauren. I also know what really happened."

"No, you don't. You don't have a fucking clue." Only her therapist knew what really happened. And Cooper. And Harris if he'd gotten into her psych files. So much for doctor/patient confidentiality.

Troy clamped his hands on her shoulders, ensuring her attention. "All Hauberk employees have to have regular psychiatric evaluations. Even the managers. Chad thinks you hold him responsible for not being able to save your daughter. Apart from his decision to protect his sister, he thinks that's why you ran from him."

She resisted the urge to press her fingers to her mouth in

horror. Did Chad truly believe she thought him responsible? "He did everything he could. I don't blame him."

Troy stepped closer, staring down at her like a judge and jury ready to pronounce sentence. "I've read your reports too."

"No. You couldn't have. Those are sealed and kept in..." Dear God, had it been Troy who had broken into the Dr. Brewer's files? Not Harris?

"You think you're the reason Emily's dead." His voice dropped to a whisper. "That if you'd just said something about what you'd been worrying about, if you'd talked to your doctor or her pediatrician you could have saved her. You think you knew there was something wrong with her, didn't you?"

"No!" Except Troy echoed what she'd wondered all this time so her denial lacked conviction. Why else had she been so obsessive about checking on Em all those months?

Grief knifed through her as sharply as it had when she'd cradled her daughter's lifeless body in her arms. If it hadn't been for Troy's hold on her, she'd have dropped to her knees.

Damn it. She'd locked that guilt away deep inside, hadn't had to face it in years. Damn him for releasing that flood gate. Needing to strike out at everything that had happened in those years—the press, Thalia's manipulations, even Chad's failure to come after her, to leave the States and fly to England, had her struggling to breathe. She flattened her hands on his chest and pushed—hard—making him stumble back. "Fuck you. You haven't a clue what you're talking about."

"Chad is still hurting. Same as you. When neither of you could have saved your daughter."

"I know that!"

"Then for Christ's sake, stop playing your stupid fucking games. Stop hiding from him. Tell Chad straight out and let him up his own mind about everything. About you. And about why you made those decisions. And where you went after you left him."

Chapter Eight

"We're positive, Chad." Sam stared out from the video chat session on Chad's laptop screen. "There's absolutely no record of an Edward Weir owning any mines in South Africa. There's no record of him coming into the country any time in the past year either. I've put out some feelers about this Light Brigade Investigators' firm Weir says he hired. They're legit as far as we can tell, and the guy I spoke to at their international office told me exactly the same story as Weir."

Chad leaned back in his chair. If this had been a setup Sam wouldn't have told him Weir hadn't checked out. He'd be telling him the threat had ramped up or something to keep him there. "I'll ask Lauren about it. She may be able to shed some light on the situation."

"Nah, tell Troy to do that. He can be in charge until we figure the rest of this shit out." Sam rolled an unlit cigar between his fingers and frowned. "I'm telling you, buddy, something's hinky about this whole set-up. I look back on it now—the phone call I got about the story on you, then Weir phoning right after? I'm thinking they were deliberately timed that way but damned if I can figure out why."

"But why? What would Weir have to gain?" Why would Lauren lie to him? No, this had to be a set-up; he just couldn't figure out their aim.

"Hey, bud?" Sam interrupted. "I hate to ask this, but is it possible Lauren's a spy for another protection agency? That maybe she's workin' for our competition and they're lookin' for a way to discredit us? Or at least discover our weaknesses?"

"If I were the competition, I wouldn't use the ex-wife of an employee. That would make them more suspicious." He'd set it up with someone they didn't know. Someone who they wouldn't suspect to be anything other than who he'd said they were, and he damned well would have made sure their cover story was in place.

Sam cursed softly. "Listen, buddy, I don't like this. I feel like a goddamned puppet being manipulated and I don't that feelin'. Why don't you head back? I'll have Sandy arrange a flight for you out of Burlington."

Puppet being manipulated. If Sam hadn't agreed to let him leave, he would have tagged Sam as the prime puppet master. So just who was pulling the strings? And why?

Chad straightened the laptop so it was aligned with the edge of the desk. "Tell Sandy I should be able to make it to Burlington by this afternoon. I still have to find Troy and tell him I'm leaving."

Sam leaned forward, his face taking up nearly the entire tiny video chat screen. "You watch your back while you're there, buddy, you hear? Tell Troy to watch his too."

"Thanks. I will." Yeah, Sam wasn't behind this. Sam would have just locked him in a room at his private club. "You know for a while there I thought maybe you and Thalia were setting me up."

"Shee-it, no." The cigar disappeared, jammed back into Sam's pocket with such force Chad was surprised the seams hadn't ripped. "No, if I wanted to do that, I would have locked you up in a room at the club until you listened to me."

Chad suppressed his smile. Did he know Sam or what?

"I would have staged a fuckin' intervention or whatever the fuck they're called," Sam continued. "I fuckin' well wouldn't have locked you in with the ice queen and hope a little global warming set in."

"You used to like her. She's the one who..." Encouraged Sam to date Jill. Ah. Strange how time and distance sometimes made things so much clearer. "She and Jill had been good friends, Sam. She was upset when she said what she did. Losing Jill right after..."—Emily— "She was confused. Upset."

"She was a self-centered bitch." A feminine gasp from off-screen told him Rosie was listening.

He lined up the pen with the mouse pad. "She needed me and I wasn't there for her. Not really. You were...collateral damage."

"She wasn't there when you needed her either, damn it. You need to get your head out of your ass and see she's not good for you. Sure, she was a good fuck, but there are lots of women who would do you in a heartbeat."

"Sam!" Rosie appeared on the screen. She hooked an arm around Sam's neck and settled in his lap. The sappy look on Sam's face should have been amusing, instead, he was jealous. "Chad, do you still love her?"

Behind her, Sam snorted and shook his head in disgust. "You see him dating anyone else lately, Rosebud? Nearly ten fuckin' years he's gone on a handful of dates with women I've set him up with. I doubt he's gone through a box of condoms that whole fuckin' time."

Rosie placed a finger over Sam's lips and ssshed him before facing the webcam again. "Chad? You need to get things straight with her. Talk to her. Listen to her." She flattened her fingers over her heart. "Listen to what your heart is telling you.

Because it sounds like you still care for her."

Behind her, Sam rolled his eyes. "Yeah, fuck her and get her out of your system. Then dump her on her ass out the front gates."

That pearl of wisdom earned Sam a slap on his hand. Damn, Sam was lucky to have convinced Rosie to come back to D.C., to agree to date him again. Just how much groveling Sam had done in New York, neither of them would say.

That's how things should have happened with him and Lauren, yet it hadn't. Which was his own damned fault. Lauren had probably expected him to fly after her and beg her to come back, the way Sam had flown after Rosie. Instead he'd let Lauren go.

"Thanks Sam. I'll phone you when I get back into D.C." Chad clicked the mouse on the "end chat" button and the chat session disappeared from the screen.

The conversation replayed in his mind as he closed up his computer. *Fuck her and get her out of your system.* Didn't Sam realize Lauren was his drug of choice? That if he fucked her again, the way he'd came too damned close to doing last night, he'd never get her out of his system?

Talk to her, Rosie had said. *Listen to her.* Right. Well, Lauren sure had some talking to do. About who Weir was and who she worked for. He just had to decide whether she'd be talking to him or to Troy for that conversation.

A quick check of her room showed Lauren hadn't returned. The closed circuit cameras revealed her location—she'd gone jogging and was a third the way out to the far end of the property. He could wait until she passed by the house and catch her then.

Ah, hell, he needed to jog this morning anyway. He lost

seven minutes dashing back up to his room and changing into his sweats. By the time he met Troy halfway out, he'd warmed up nicely. Both his muscles and his irritation.

Troy slowed as he approached Chad. "If you're looking for Lauren, she's up the hill."

Once again he debated turning around and waiting for her to return to the house but decided against it. If it ended up with her screaming at him again, he'd rather do it where no one could hear. He found her pounding hell bent for leather down the path.

"Lauren."

She glanced over her shoulder but kept running. "Leave me alone right now, Chad. I'm not very good company."

His step hesitated as he almost did turn around. No, if someone was trying to discredit Hauberk through her, he owed it to Sam—and Troy—to find out just what the hell was going on.

"Lauren, slow down, damn it."

She didn't.

He sprinted, thinking he was fresher and could take advantage of her exhaustion. Considering she'd probably run close to five kilometers already, it still took a concerted effort to catch up. "You're worn out and if you keep this up, you're going to trip over a root and twist your ankle." Not to mention he needed to talk to her face-to-face instead of to her ass, as nice a view as that was.

With a huff of exasperation, most likely more at herself than at him, Lauren slowed down and a few hundred yards up stopped entirely. Breathing hard, she braced her hands on her knees.

"Just leave me alone for a while. Please."

"That's not what you were begging me to do last night. Or have you forgotten how you got on your knees and sucked my dick?" *Fuck. That was a stupid—*

Before he could finish the thought, Lauren did a neat sweep with her foot he wasn't expecting and he found himself flat on his back, the breath driven from him. He rolled to a stand and watched her disappear down the trail.

So she wanted to play it that way, did she? Game on.

They ran half the trail dodging and evading each other's attacks. At some point, he couldn't figure out when, his anger morphed to arousal. He found himself admiring that she'd run more than twice as far as he had yet showed no signs of tiring; he also found himself admiring the swing of her hips as she ran in front of him, the bounce of her breasts when they wrestled. Until they reached the steep hill and she stumbled over a protruding root as he'd predicted would happen. Launching himself at her, Chad trapped her by using his full weight on top of her.

She fought him for a moment, attempting to buck him off, then relaxed. Chuckling, she reached up and skimmed a finger down his jaw. "You still get turned on by the chase, don't you?"

Considering the erection jabbing into her belly he could hardly deny it.

"Never could understand guys who liked submissive women." He ground his cock against her mound then, with a sigh, sat back on his heels but stayed straddling her. "You realize my guys are probably watching on the monitors."

"They even have cameras out here?"

He tipped his head toward the gazebo further down the path. "There are a couple mounted down there. They're motion activated and we're within range."

"Shit." She shoved him off and scrambled to her feet. "What

did you want that you had to chase me for this far?"

He opened his mouth to say "I'm leaving" but the words wouldn't come. The sensual side she'd shown him yesterday, the *I want you. I've only ever wanted you* hunger in her eyes had returned.

"Yesterday you said we needed to talk. I told you we'd talk this morning." Talk? He wanted to bend her over the trunk of that fallen tree and fuck her from behind. He took a deep breath and centered himself. "I told you not to leave your room without me, or are you incapable of following orders?"

She straightened, holding her chin high. "I brought my gun and one of your guards. It was only a matter of time before I returned." Her eyes narrowed. "Besides, Hauberk guaranteed this as a safe house and their employees as well-trained professionals. Are you telling me this place isn't secure?"

"We can't—oh, for Christ's sakes, just come with me." Chad stalked down the path toward the pond, wondering if she would indeed follow him. He made it almost to the gazebo before he chanced a glance back and realize she still stood there, her shoulders slumped. "Don't play any more games with me, Lauren."

"I wasn't playing a—" Her voice fractured and she cleared her throat. If it were anyone else, he'd think she was fighting tears, but her eyes were dry.

"You were sleeping when I checked on you this morning," she continued, her voice firm once again. "I know you were up late last night so I didn't want to disturb you." When he didn't say anything, she explained, "I saw the light under your door, that's how I know you were up until at least four this morning."

Which meant she'd been awake too. Plotting a sob story? No, that wasn't Lauren's style. There were circles beneath her eyes he realized as he took a closer look, lending her an air of fragility that belied her defiance. He reminded himself all wasn't what it appeared. "I've got some questions for you."

She opened her mouth as if to snap something in return but instead she simply sighed. "Fine."

Fine. Now there was a landmine of a word.

His hand firm on her elbow, he followed her up the wooden steps leading to the gazebo overlooking the pond and the rest of the valley. He steered her to the canopied sofa where she sank onto the cushions with a soul deep sigh.

She'd run hard, worked up a sweat so her T-shirt clung to her curves, making him acutely aware of the hard nipples jutting from the fabric. Except for the Sig Sauer in its holster, she was the ultimate picture of femininity and composure, her feet neatly crossed at the ankles, her hands clasped on her lap. *Concentrate on the mission, damn it.*

Instead of folding his arms the way he wanted to, he let them hang loose and leaned against the center post in an attempt to appear relaxed. "I want to talk about why you're here."

"Okay."

"You work for a private investigation firm called Light Brigade Investigations, Inc."

Her gaze met his for just a second before it flitted away to focus on something on the other side of the pond. "Yes."

"They sent you to South Africa to determine if a mole in Edward Weir's mining company was selling corporate secrets."

"Yes." If he hadn't been watching her carefully, he may not have noticed her fingernails dig into the skin of her knuckles. Or the almost imperceptible tightening of her shoulders.

She'd just lied. Why?

"And you uncovered someone who led you to a man named

Frank Harris."

"Yes."

Chad swore under his breath. "If you keep giving me one word answers, we'll be here all frickin' day. Don't you want us to catch whoever it is who has forced you to hide?" *Tell me why you're really here.*

He continued questioning until he'd verified her story corroborated with Weir's. Which of course it did, damn it. The silence between them hung heavy, as if someone had hung a blanket between them. It wasn't that he didn't have questions for her. The big one, the *Why are you lying?* one got shoved aside by the others crowding his mind. *Where have you been? Why didn't you call me, tell me where you were going when you moved from London? Or Paris?*

A damned email might have been nice. A text message. Something. Anything to let me know you were all right.

Did you know I still dream about you? About us? He heaved in a breath and found himself staring at a spot across the lake, absently wondering if they were staring at the same tree. Damn it, this was the reason why ex-husbands should never be assigned to guard their ex-wives.

Focus on your mission. Which was...what? Was she in danger? Or was this some sort of setup to discredit Hauberk?

He lost track of the time they'd been there when she suddenly spoke, startling him. "I suppose you guessed I haven't been living in London for a while now."

"Yes." Any of his attempts to contact her had gone unanswered so he'd used his Hauberk resources to track her. "You ran the security for a fancy spa, Tranquil Pastures or something, for six months in Kent, then quit and moved to Brussels. Six months after that you moved to Paris where you were hired to guard the wife and children of a Saudi Arabian family."

Her gaze darted back to him before returning to the pond. "You've got good sources."

Not good enough. From there, she'd dropped from his radar. "And now you work out of your company's offices in Rome."

"Yes."

He shoved his hands in his pockets and walked to the stop of the stairs, blocking the exit. "Did you know there's no record of an Edward Weir owning any mine, diamond, gold or otherwise, in South Africa? Or anywhere in Africa, Australia, Canada or the States?"

"He's not the only owner, so the mine isn't in his name. It's registered to a numbered off-shore corporation." She finally looked at him, her mask of composure firmly in place.

"Did you also know that there's no record of him coming into the country in the past six months? Oh, there were several Edward Weirs but none fitting your boss's description."

Once again that spot across the pond got her undivided attention. "Maybe you aren't looking in the right places."

Why was every nerve ending twitching? Oh, yeah, because she was *lying*.

"I've spoken with Sam, Lauren. Yesterday morning he got a call from someone at the Post telling him about a spread they'd be running about me, about...back then. Sort of a 'where are they now and how did they change American history' type story. Ten minutes later Weir phoned Sam. Told him he'd be coming into the office, laid out what he needed. Not once did he mention you by name. But he knew we'd been married, didn't he?"

"Yes." He could hardly hear her whisper above the wind in

the trees.

"They went through the various operatives Sam thought could run the operation and Weir found fault with every single operative. Except me."

"Because you are the best. Because you're the only one I trust."

He dismissed that as flattery. Or prevarication. She hadn't trusted him all those years before. "You know it's never SOP to assign an ex-spouse as a bodyguard. There's too much baggage attached." The truckloads they had between them could fill Chesapeake Bay. "So, what's the story? Is there someone after you? Or is this some elaborate scheme to discredit Hauberk?"

"There really is a threat." This time she looked at him, her hands were still together in her lap, but her fingernails no longer scored the skin. Her expression was composed if rather sad, not tense. Her shoulders slumped, and a hint of vulnerability pierced her armor. "LBI caters to very rich clients who need discreet investigations—blackmail, that type of thing. I'd investigated this scumbag who was blackmailing a certain high profile movie star. Part of the fallout of it was the scumbag's wife divorced him. I had taken some incriminating pictures of him as part of my investigation and so I was called to testify against him at his wife's petition for full custody. Which she got based mainly on my testimony. Next thing we knew he'd hired Harris."

When he'd first met her, she'd been quick with a retort, her eyes sparkling, her mouth pulling up at the ends in the most provocative grin he'd ever seen. They'd laughed at lot in those early years. Before. Even in their more serious moments, they were in tune—finishing each other's sentences, knowing when the other needed a touch, gentle or not, to ground them. For a while there, things had been so good between them he'd have taken a bet that their marriage could have survived anything.

What he'd give to see her smile. Just once. The way she had...before. The memory of finding her on her knees, sobbing, clutching Emily's lifeless body. Of the tears streaming down her face at the funeral. Tears that dried up and never reappeared. She'd held herself in ruthless control after that. She'd closed herself off from him and everyone.

He shook his head and forced himself to focus on his objective. Damn it, why the hell was he still so attracted to her? *Concentrate on the mission. Stop letting her distract you.* This was the very reason he shouldn't have been put in charge of the op. "So, who's Weir?"

"Ed's my partner. Or, he was my partner. I've told my boss that once this is settled, I'm quitting."

"Why come to Hauberk? Couldn't your own people protect you?"

"LBI's a small company. We don't have the type of safe houses Hauberk does, or the manpower to protect me. Harris is...dangerous."

"So you manipulated Sam and me until I was assigned as your lead op."

She nodded.

"So there's no story in the Post this weekend? You had someone call it in to convince Sam to assign me to your case?"

"No, there really a story. Ed's sister works for the Post so we knew they were working on it."

Shit. He grabbed the pine railing and stared over the lake. "Why me, Lauren? Why seek me out after all these years?"

"Because you're not the type of man to walk away from an assignment. Because I trust you."

From the location of her voice, she'd moved. Was coming

closer.

His shoulders stiffened as if he were expecting her to plunge yet another metaphorical knife between them. “You didn’t trust me when we were married. Why in hell would you trust me now?”

The footsteps stopped. “I trusted you! I’ve always trusted you.”

He snorted. “You trusted me not to follow you to England.”

She’d been right. He’d let her walk away. Until yesterday he’d questioned that decision every day. Now, with her here, he wasn’t sure that perhaps it hadn’t been the best decision he’d ever made. The ability to live with the hole she’d left had been torn from him and when this was over, he’d have to rebuild everything all over again.

“I didn’t leave you because I didn’t trust you. I left because I trusted the wrong person’s advice. I made a bad decision, Chad. Haven’t you ever made a decision you regretted later?”

Instead of feeling the satisfaction, the relief he’d expected, anger surged inside him, a low burn that boiled over. “It’s taken you nearly ten years—ten fucking years—to find me to tell me that? You threw everything we had together away, Lauren. I gave you my word that I would be there for you. I stood up in front of a judge and promised to love, honor and cherish you, no matter what. So did you.”

“I know. I should have stayed.” Her quiet answer slipped into his brain, into his heart, a soothing balm tipped with barbs. “I was mixed up; I wasn’t thinking clearly. By the time I realized it, I thought you’d moved on.”

“I loved you, Lauren.” Part of him still did no matter how much he tried to deny it. “I would have done anything to make our marriage work.”

She slipped past him and leaned against the door post, her

arms wrapped around her waist the only clue that she wasn't as composed as she tried to appear. "I'm sorry. I'm sorry about not trusting you, about not talking to you—not telling you what was going on in my head."

Did her apology help ease the hurt? He did a mental check. Nope. That goddamned ache in his chest still hurt like a sonovabitch.

He forced himself to look at her without allowing her to see how much her apology hurt. He'd be damned if he'd give her that power over him. "I'm going back to D.C. Troy can—"

"Please. Don't leave." She moved closer, her breasts brushing his shirt, her hips touching his. She hadn't put on any perfume but there was still a hint of something fruity wafting from her, probably her shampoo.

His cock punched a tent in the front of his sweats. Fuck.

"Don't leave. Not with this still between us," she whispered. "I thought I was doing the right thing. Once I realized what a mess I'd made of things, I'd been told you were already with someone else and I figured it was better to let you go."

God, he wanted to touch her. To hold her. To have her rest her head against his shoulder the way she had the night before. While his brain was saying "damned straight I didn't understand," his cock was saying "lie down on the couch, babe, and let me taste you again." At the moment, it was a dead heat as to which body part would win the argument. Then his guts weighed in. When this was over—whatever *it* was—would he find himself alone? Because there was no way he could go through losing her again.

"How would you know if I was with someone else? You were half the fuckin' world away." Maybe if he couldn't smell her he could fight whatever spell she was weaving. Distance, that's what he needed. Yet he couldn't move; his legs felt like they'd been nailed in place. "What do you want from me, Lauren?"

"*From* you? Nothing. But I need to make things right for you, for both of us," she whispered. Her eyes slowly lifted to his again. He lost himself in the flecks of gold buried amongst the brown. "I want to...I want us to try again."

His hand reached for her, hovered an inch above her hair before he stopped himself. Damn, she looked just like she did when they were first dating. When they'd finally admitted what they'd each needed, wanted from the other. On their wedding day when she'd promised to love him for better or worse. Well, he sure as hell had delivered the worst, hadn't he?

She looked up at him, conviction firm in her voice as well as her eyes. "I'll do whatever you ask to prove myself to you. Except leave."

"Will you?" He gave in to the temptation and touched her hair with one finger. It was as soft, as silky as he remembered. He cupped the back of her head, holding her in place, letting her feel his control. A dark wave of lust swamped him. Why not make her prove she'd changed? Or not. Why not satisfy that demon inside that needed to punish her? He tightened his grip. "If I told you to suck me off right here where my men could see you, would you do it?"

"Yes." There was no hesitation to her answer. She started to reach for his waistband.

What the hell was he doing? They were out in the open where anyone could see. He had to work with these men, command their respect, not give them a thrill watching their boss get a blowjob. "Stop."

"But..."

Telling his dick it would just have to wait, he stepped out of her reach. "You want to do something for me? You want me to trust you? Then stop lying to me and tell me the truth. About what the hell the threat is and exactly why you're here."

They stared at each other for a long moment, the faint buzz of a plane thirty thousand feet above and a sparrow chirping to his mate the only sounds breaking the silence. Finally she nodded. "All right, but I can't tell you everything. Some of it's classified."

Classified? Perhaps this Light Brigade place she'd worked for had involved one of the alphabet agencies if Harris had terrorist connections. "Come on, let's go back to the house. I'd rather not have anyone listen in to whatever we end up saying."

Or watch whatever they ended up doing. Be it yelling or making love.

Chapter Nine

The two of them walked along the path back to the house without speaking. While they walked, Chad wondered if Lauren was composing answers for him with the same deliberation he was preparing his questions. For years he'd been composing what he wanted to ask. Yet so many of the questions now seemed futile or petty. She'd walked away from him. She'd been clear she hadn't agreed with his decision about the FBI. She'd been furious when that video of the two of them having sex in their bedroom had been posted on the internet and gone viral, how stills had been splashed across every goddamned newspaper on the east coast and beyond. To this day he hadn't figured out how someone had managed to sneak a camera into the house. He'd gone over the place with every detector he could lay his hands on and never found a trace of the goddamned thing.

He'd done every damned thing she'd asked. Yet it hadn't been enough. The sense of hope that had flared to life twisted on him, turned into a serpent intent on destroying his dreams.

Once they were in her room and he'd closed the door, Lauren took a deep breath and faced him. "I really am sorry. About leaving you. I know it was wrong. I apologize for that."

"You've said that already." He scrubbed his hands over his face as he fought for control. "Look, I know you were unhappy. I know you didn't agree with some of the choices I made. Thalia told me—"

"Let's not talk about Thalia right now." The bleakness in her eyes sucker punched him, driving away the righteous indignation that had plagued him just moments before. "Even before Emily's death, I was pretty messed up. There was something wrong with me, about the way I watched Emily."

What had he missed?

He thought back on those months, of watching her nursing Emily, cuddling her, sleeping with her right beside their bed, her hand often resting on their daughter as the two of them slept. "Babe, you were the best mother a baby could ever ask for. You were always there with Emily. You carried her everywhere you went. I know. I saw you."

"From the day we brought Em home from the hospital, I was terrified to go to sleep." Her voice cracked. "I was afraid if I did, she'd stop breathing and I wouldn't know."

How could that be? How could he not have seen that she'd been afraid? Then again he'd been at work during the day, a lot of evenings too. Especially that last month when he and his team had been winding up that inside trading investigation. Had he neglected his family because of a goddamned greedy banker?

"During the day, when you were at work, I'd keep her in her carry seat, so I could take her with me everywhere. I was afraid to leave her alone." Her voice was a toneless whisper. "Then one day, she turned over on her own."

He remembered that day. She'd called him with the news but he'd had to cut her off because they were in the middle of a meeting. She'd been upset with him that night—at the time he'd thought she was angry because she felt he'd blown her off. Had it been fear driving her anger? "That's one of the signs she was growing up, Lauren. It meant she was healthy, that's all."

"They told us at our Lamaze classes we shouldn't let the baby sleep on her stomach, remember?" He stayed very still, afraid to jar her from her trance-like recitation. "After that, I was terrified. How was I supposed to stop her from rolling over on her stomach if I fell asleep?" She closed her eyes for a moment and took another deep breath. When she opened them again, her voice was steadier, controlled. At what cost? "I'd sit on the side of the bed with my hand on her, making sure she was breathing. Sometimes I'd watch her all night."

Oh, God, it was right in front of him and he hadn't seen it.

"I knew something was wrong with me, but I couldn't do anything, I couldn't say anything to anyone. I just kept hoping you'd see it. That you'd see what was happening and do something. Take me to the doctor or something."

"Why didn't say something? Tell me? I would have helped you."

"Because I was afraid. I was terrified they'd say I was an unfit mother. That you'd take Emily away from me."

"I would never have taken her from you, babe. You loved her more than life itself." He couldn't help himself; he wrapped his arms about her and drew her close, stroking up and down her spine, gently, comforting the way she liked.

"That night. You came home late, remember?" Her whole body shuddered in his arms. "You'd wrapped some case up and got your promotion."

Oh, shit, and she'd fallen asleep after they'd made love. Had she never fallen asleep after the way he did? "Is that why you said it was my fault Emily...died?"

She took a deep shuddering breath, giving him the impression that she was ready to shatter. "Don't you see? If I'd been awake, I might have noticed that she'd stopped breathing.

I might have been able to save her. I know it wasn't your fault, but I wasn't thinking straight and I..."

"It wasn't your fault. You know that. It wasn't anyone's fault." Here he'd been blaming himself, thinking Lauren had blamed him for Emily's death, and she'd been blaming herself. They'd both carried too much crap around for too long.

Her words were muffled but controlled. "Maybe I sensed something but just didn't realize it. If I'd said something, they could have tested her. Put her on one of those apnea blankets that monitored her breathing. If she'd been on one of those, the alarm would have gone off and we could have saved her."

Her head shook against his shoulder and he realized there was a damp patch on it. She was crying without making a sound. He held her tightly against him, stroking her back. "You can't second guess yourself, babe." He wore the crown of perfect vision hindsight after Thalia's shooting. He pulled Lauren away and cradled her face in his palms. Tears streaked down her face. He brushed his thumb over her cheek, wiping them from their tracks. "Emily had none of the indicators—she wasn't premature, she had no physical signs to make us suspect she'd stop breathing. You know that."

Lauren started to say something but he cut her off. "You read the autopsy report, Lauren. You know what the coroner said. You didn't do anything wrong. Neither of us did."

"I'm sorry," she whispered, her voice hoarse, as if she'd been shouting for hours. Her deep shuddering sigh echoed through his bones and settled into his soul.

He continued to stroke her cheek as the tears slowed. "So you ran to England?"

To Tranquil Pastures...which was a fancy name for a private clinic specializing in treating people having...mental difficulties. Oh, God. "You weren't in charge of security at that spa, were you?"

"No. I was a patient."

"Why didn't you tell me? Why not find something local?" Somewhere I could have visited you. Helped you.

"Thalia found the place for me. I told her I wanted it to be somewhere private so no one could find out that I was there. The press were already tearing you apart. I didn't want anyone to go after you because I was so weak." The press had been in a feeding frenzy and were pointing the fingers at him as the poster child of how the FBI had failed the country. What woman—especially one recovering from the death of her child—voluntarily put themselves into a spotlight like that? He wondered who had been advising her. His lawyers perhaps? Or Thalia?

And why the fuck hadn't Thalia told him where Lauren was or what she'd been going through? He didn't need to ask how his sister had raised the money. He had a damned good idea where it had come from—she'd been millionaire Cooper Davis's lover at the time. But however she'd gotten ahold of the cash, his sister was due for a long talk about boundaries, and secret keeping, and interfering between a husband and wife.

He started at the ceiling for a second before shaking his head and looking at her. "I get that you needed help. That you needed to get away from the press. From everything." His voice had thickened so he cleared his throat. "What I don't understand is why you stayed away for so long. Without a phone call. A letter. Something. Anything."

"I did write to you," Lauren said in confusion. "I wrote to you a couple weeks after I left, explaining where I was, begging your forgiveness. I wrote week after week. Asking you if I could come back when I was released. But you never replied. So when I got out, I didn't think you wanted me back."

"I didn't get any letters, Lauren. Not one."

He'd hadn't seen her letters? Oh, dear God, had Thalia been intercepting his mail? But on which end? At the spa or their condo? "I sent dozens."

He shook his head.

"I should have come back right then, shouldn't I?" She sighed. So many mistakes she'd made. Too many. "Then, one day, your lawyer showed up on my doorstep with the divorce papers. I took that as your answer, so I signed them." She debated telling him about Thalia's role, but decided against it. He'd figure it out soon enough. The conversation needed to be about them, not his sister.

"*My* lawyer showed up with the divorce papers?" His eyes closed and he canted his head back as he drew in a deep breath. When he looked at her again, his expression was shuttered. "You divorced me, Lauren. Not the other way around. I'm the one who got served."

"No, I didn't seek the divorce. I'd wanted to come home, to try again. I swear." Dear God, he didn't believe her. Lauren's legs wouldn't support her; she slumped onto the bed. "The solicitor said he represented your lawyers here in the States. He said you were living with someone else. That you wanted the divorce so you could marry her."

"What was the solicitor's name?" Chad's voice was soft, but she heard the menace underlying it.

She told him, wondering just what Chad would do to him. Destroy his career? Or have him met in a dark corner someplace to mete out his own form of vengeance?

"It wasn't until a few weeks ago that I discovered you'd never remarried." *That you weren't the one who had hired the lawyer.*

His breath escaped him in a huff; he looked to the side. "I kept hoping you'd come back. I bought a house and fixed it up. So if you came back I could offer you somewhere better to live than our condo. And I own forty-nine percent of Hauberk, Lauren. Sam's my partner, not my boss." The look he gave her was so bleak her chest ached. "I did it for you, Lauren. I know I fucked up with the FBI. I know you were disappointed with me for going against orders, that you didn't think I'd be able to provide for you anymore. I needed to prove to you that I could still be someone you could rely on."

"I never thought that. Oh, God, Chad, I never ever thought that of you. I know why you went against orders. I understand that. I always did." She closed the distance between them and wrapped her arms about his waist. "I didn't leave you because of that."

His arms banded around her, holding her tight against him. How long they stood there she couldn't say. Eventually he took a deep breath and placed his hands on her shoulders, pulling her away.

"We've both made mistakes. That ends now. We say whatever we feel, we don't shut the other out and expect them to know what we're thinking. Agreed?"

She nodded. Half of her hoped Harris wouldn't be found for months. Hell, ninety-nine-point-nine percent of her hoped Harris would never be found. They could live here forever, safe.

Chad wrapped his arms around Lauren and pulled her against him once more. She sighed with a quiet moan as she softened against him.

This was the way it was supposed to be. The two of them together, damn the world outside. If she hadn't sought the divorce the way he'd believed, and she hadn't left...was there hope for them?

There was so much time to make up, so many nights he'd been alone with only his own hand to satisfy his needs. The nights he'd spent on duty at the club, watching everyone else having sex hadn't helped. In the years they'd been together, she'd known how to turn him on, known that he didn't like a passive woman but a willing partner. Her heart hammered against his chest, her breath warmed his cheek in a gentle caress, her hips ground against his erection.

He lowered his head and caught her lips in a kiss, one with enough pressure that she'd know exactly what he expected.

Her fingernails digging into his biceps was his first clue that she remembered. And that she'd give him exactly what he needed. He damned near swore when her grip on him ceased until his sweat pants slid down his legs to pool at his ankles. She broke the kiss and sank to her knees.

Was there anything as erotic as watching her tongue dart out to dampen her lips, or the smoky look in her eyes as she stared at his erection?

Her mouth closed over the swollen tip and he had to say yes, having her mouth sucking his cock was a lot more fucking erotic. Her tongue slid up the length of his shaft and her hand circled the base in a loose fist.

"Suck it down, babe. You know how I like it."

She did. God, her mouth hadn't lost any of its skill. She used just the right pressure with her tongue, her teeth rasped just the right spots and the suction that hollowed out her cheeks...holy fucking shit. Her free hand slipped around his ass, cupping one of his cheeks. When she started humming, the vibration shot straight down his shaft and landed in his balls.

He groaned from deep in his belly and wrapped his fingers in her hair. She rocked against him, taking him deep until the head hit the soft palate at the back of her mouth, then withdrew. She repeated the movement until he clung to her as if the room was spinning. His eyelids weighed a ton. He fought them from closing. If they did, she might disappear and he'd wake up to find this was all a dream.

The familiar tingle started in his balls, drawing them up tight against this body and he stopped her. "On the bed, babe. I need to finish inside you."

She withdrew, taking the time to press a kiss to the end of his glistening shaft in a gesture so sweet, so gentle, he wanted to gather her in his arms and just hold her. How had he ever let her just walk away? Why hadn't he flown to London to visit her, to find out... No, he told himself. Those days were past, and while he knew there were questions still to be answered, this was not the time. If nothing else came of this reunion, he'd have the memory of her beneath him, around him one last time.

A frown creased her forehead. "I should have a shower. I'm all sweaty."

"So am I. I don't care." He pulled his T-shirt over his head and dropped it on his sweat pants then reached for her shirt.

Their clothes on the floor seconds later, Lauren stretched out on the bed, propping herself up on the pillows. His chest tightened as her hand smoothed over her belly and she parted her folds and began to play with herself. His cock ached to be inside her, especially when she let her legs fall open and gave him a glimpse of her glistening pussy. Shit, she knew how he loved watching her get herself off. But watching would have to wait.

He crawled up the bed and wedged himself between her thighs. God, he'd loved how she smelled, how she tasted. Her scent had lingered in the closet for a few weeks, no more, and he'd mourned when it had faded. He buried his face in her mound and inhaled, filling his lungs with her.

Ignoring the need to continue his path up her body, he stayed right where he was. He deserved the chance to reacquaint himself with this part of her body. Besides, while he was primed and ready, she'd had no foreplay at all.

He nuzzled lower until her essence coated his lips. Her taste burst on his tongue like a ripened peach. He swirled his tongue through her cream, alternately lapping and teasing until he found the tiny bundle of nerves. Her hips rose off the mattress but he clamped down, holding her in place.

He'd intended to hold off on finding his own pleasure until she'd come for him twice, but she moaned that deep-throated gasp that forewarned him of an impending orgasm and all his plans flew out the window. He found himself over her, his cock poised at her entrance. Her legs wrapped about his thighs and drew him close until he was buried to the hilt inside her.

None of his dreams, none of his memories, matched the sheer heaven of being surrounded by her heat. He stared down at her, wanting to order her to open her eyes, to watch them unfocus as she came. But there was something ethereal about the look on her face that made him hold off. He didn't need to see her eyes when her body told her everything he needed to know. Her swollen lips were parted, tiny puffs of air as she gasped for breath warmed his arm when she turned her head, unseeing, toward it. Her body rippled around him, drawing him in deeper. Her hips undulated, grinding her clit with each pass. Her nipples were hard dark berries, larger than they had been when they were first married, softer too, from age and breast feeding but they were just as beautiful.

He dipped his head and caught one between his teeth. He wanted to crow when her pussy clamped tight around him. When this was over he'd ask her about the scar on the inside of her arm that looked like a burn or the one on her hip where a bullet had gone in one fleshy side and out the other. For now, he'd celebrate that they were here. Together.

He rocked his hips back then pushed back in, balls deep. His own eyes closed as he set a steady rhythm, until he could control himself no more. Her heels dug into his behind and her nails dug into his biceps as she came silently. When he followed her seconds later, he wasn't so quiet, his hoarse roar echoing off the walls.

It took him a moment before he could rouse himself to roll off her. As soon as he was on the mattress beside her, Lauren rolled into his arms with a murmured, "I love you" that had him burying his face in her hair.

Maybe they could make it work. For the first time in years, hope replaced the dark pressure in his heart.

Chapter Ten

Lauren awoke to find Chad wrapped around her the way he had for the last four nights. Like each previous morning, his hand rested on her breast while his erection prodded her hip. "Mmm, that's a nice way to wake up."

"Just relax, babe. Let me do all the work." The heat of his breath on her skin was the only warning she got before he sucked her nipple into his mouth. He spent a few minutes toying with her, his teeth rasping over her delicate flesh, occasionally tugging with a sharp nip, then his tongue would soothe the sting until she was panting.

She shifted, with every intention of touching him, but her hands wouldn't move. Another tug confirmed it—he'd restrained her wrists above her head while she slept. Had he restrained her ankles too? She wiggled her feet. Nope. Well, this should be...interesting.

Squinting, she opened her eyes, letting them adjust to the bright sunlight slanting across the bed that painted his skin pure gold. "You mind telling me just how long you plan on keeping me here?"

Tell me "forever".

He lifted his head and looked at her, a wolfish look in his eyes and a smile tugging at his lips. "I don't plan on loosening those restraints until I've made you come at least three times."

"You've always loved a challenge."

He set to his task, using his mouth and his hands to rediscover all the places that drove her crazy—the spot on her neck directly beneath her ear, the soft skin inside her elbow, just above each hip. She closed her eyes and gave in to the erotic sensation of his breath and his mouth on her. He explored every inch of her body until she was panting, aching with need.

Finally he parted her folds with his thumbs. His tongue traced where his thumbs had been, flicking over her clit with a light touch.

"I've always loved how you taste, Lauren." When they'd been married and he said that, there had been pride in his voice, but now...now there was need, heat, urgency. And something else. Not anger, but... determination? Whether to prove something to her or to him, she didn't even try to guess. Before she could decide how she felt, he returned to his task. Her orgasm slammed into her like a tidal wave, lifting her hips from the mattress as her pussy sought to be filled.

He planted his hands on either side of her head and eased into her. She lost herself in the familiarity of the scene. Of his scent, his rhythm. Him surrounding her. Filling her. The sounds of flesh on flesh, their breathing as it quickened, became her whole world. *This. This is what I've searched for. This is what I missed, what I've wanted.*

He'd just collapsed on top of her, both having found their release, when someone knocked at Chad's bedroom door.

"Do you think if we're quiet they'll go away?" she whispered. She felt Chad's snort more than heard it.

The handle to Chad's door rattled. On the far side there was a quiet curse, then whoever it was pounded on her door. "Get your butt out here, Miller." Troy. Shit. "Sam's on the phone."

"All right, I'm coming," Chad called in return.

"Not anymore," Lauren said beneath her breath. Even exhausted from their lovemaking as she was, she couldn't help but admire his butt when he rolled out of bed and headed to the bathroom.

When he returned, he leaned against the doorframe. She tugged on the restraints still binding her to the headboard. "Do you mind letting me go? I could use a trip to the bathroom myself."

Her chest hurt at the predatory satisfaction of the smile he gave her. "I'm not sure. I'm not done yet, am I?"

"What do you mean?"

"I told you I'd make you come three times and by my count you've only come twice."

"You always were an overachiever." Her breath caught when he leaned down to kiss her. Without breaking the kiss, he freed her, allowing her to wrap her arms around his neck. They were both breathing heavily before he broke away. "Promise me you'll come back and give me a chance to even the score?"

"I won't be long. And I will definitely be back. You can count on it."

"Chad." Troy pounded on the door again. "Get your ass out here before I break the effin' door, damn it."

He returned to his room and closed the adjoining door. Lauren swung from the bed and padded to the bathroom. When she returned, the connecting door was open once again. Instead of Chad, Troy stood in the middle of the room, his expression guarded as his gaze raked the length of her.

"Well, well, well. Looks like Father Christmas arrived early—or late—this year. You look good with your hair all messed up like that. The razor burn on your chest is a nice touch too."

She headed to the closet to grab a robe, then stopped. Chad had said he would be right back and she was damned if she'd let Troy stop him from giving her that third orgasm. Instead she grabbed the top sheet off the bed and wrapped it around her toga style. "Where's Chad?"

"Talking to Sam on the encrypted system downstairs. He'll be back in a bit." His gaze met hers finally, his expression hard. "The longer you play kissy-face while lying to him, the worse it's going to hurt him when he finds out the truth. Just get it over with—tell him. Tell him everything.

"He knows about why I was at the spa."

"Good." He nodded in approval. "Then tell him the rest. About the Brigade, about Thalia's part in committing you to that asylum

She stilled. "You know what she did?"

"I overheard that fight you had with her, remember? About how she'd told you Chad had remarried." Troy had been the one who had told her Chad barely even dated. "I also told you, I got into your files, remember? After I read yours, I read hers."

"Oh."

"You need to tell him, Lauren. He needs to know."

"What am I supposed to say? 'By the way, Chad, your sister is a lying bitch who manipulated me and I was so stupid I let her'?"

"He deserves the truth, damn it. Not many men these days live with the type of code he holds himself and others to. If you want to keep him, you'll effin' come clean to him. He deserves that much after what he's given up for you both. He gave up his career to protect her."

"Going against orders was his choice." The hurt, the betrayal she'd felt when she'd learned what he'd done raked her again. Not that he'd gone against them, but that he hadn't talked to her first. But even if she'd known, what would she have said or done? "He could have asked her to stop going to that damned place until Vandeburg was captured."

"He had. She refused."

Lauren stilled. "He never told me."

Troy sighed. "All right, so save Thalia for later. For Christ's sake, at least tell him who Cooper really is and have him banned from that damned club before he brings trouble to its doors. That's the last thing either Sam or Chad need after sacrificing their careers for it."

"Yes, Lauren. Tell me who Cooper really is. Tell me why he should be banned from his own club."

Her own expression couldn't have looked any less guilty than Troy's when they both stared at Chad, who stood in the connecting doorway.

Tension radiated from him as he stalked into the room, his fingers flexing as if they wanted to go for his weapon. Or punch Troy in the jaw. When he looked at her, the warmth that had been in them just minutes before had been replaced with ice.

"Who the hell is Cooper, Lauren? What's he doing that should get him banned from the club?" Chad repeated.

Troy's shoulders slumped; he ran a hand through his thick mane of hair. "Cooper's running—"

"Troy, stop," Lauren interrupted, sensing he was quite willing to throw her to the wolves. "I'm sorry, Chad, but Troy can't tell you anything about it. You need to forget what you just heard."

The glare he turned on her could have withered a nun's

wimple. "Like hell I'm going to forget what I heard. Now, you tell me what Cooper's up to."

"We can't."

"You *won't,*" Chad corrected.

"No, I mean we can't. I signed a secrecy agreement."

"What'll happen if you break that agreement? You'll be slapped on the wrist? Fired? You've told me you've already quit." His voice could have frozen the Potomac in July. "What the hell is he doing? Is Cooper the man you were investigating? Is he the one who hired Harris?"

When she didn't answer, he yelled, "Tell me, damn it!"

"Cooper was my boss. That's all I can tell you. And even that can get us all in trouble."

Troy apparently didn't feel the same boundaries. "Fuck that. Cooper is head of The Brigade. It's a multi-government, black-op, hostage rescue unit that operates separately from any of the government agencies in order to provide plausible deniability."

Chapter Eleven

Chad jerked back as if he'd been shot. He straightened and looked between the two of them, processing the various scenarios from the little information he'd gleaned and added it to his conversation with Sam. "You lied to me. Both of you."

"We had to," Lauren agreed quietly. "The Brigade often has to infiltrate terrorist organizations. If the wrong piece of information gets out, if the wrong person finds out about something, people could die. If we talk to someone who we're not authorized to talk to, we can be charged with treason and tried in a very private court with a very private—and very final—sentence."

His stomach felt as if he'd been buckled into a roller coaster that was doing loops and spins, ready to rocket off its rails. He hated roller coasters.

He glanced at Troy, who was staring stone-faced out the window. "How long have you known about this?"

"About eight months. It was the Brigade who extracted our guys in Colombia." Troy slumped on the windowsill. "Lauren was running the op. I don't remember seeing Weir there, but things got pretty hairy and...well, maybe he was there and I just missed him."

"Does Sam know about any of this?"

"No."

Which explained why Troy had worked from home for weeks after he'd returned from Colombia.

The roller coaster they were riding flipped over in a dozen different directions then abruptly stopped. She'd owed him no explanation. If she'd been working with a black ops team, she wouldn't have been able to tell him anything. They'd each had to keep certain parts of their work secret from each other before. How was this any different?

Troy was a different matter. He may have possibly put not only Hauberk but the club members at risk. However there was nothing to be done about it at the moment. Not until they'd solved this current situation.

"Is there really a threat? Is there really a Jack Harris?"

"Yes, there's really a Jack Harris. He's after me because I had him taken off active duty. And you're a target because he may try to get back at me by hitting you."

Could he believe her? She'd given him a completely different story in the gazebo. Was this tale any closer to the truth than that one? "Who is he really?"

"He's a former British agent. He'd been working undercover to infiltrate an offshoot of the Shining Path when his cover got blown. He didn't like the way his government handled his case after he got back so Cooper recruited him."

"Why did you have him taken off active duty?"

She took a deep breath. "I can't tell you everything, but I can tell you we noticed he was having problems after a mission went sour in Somalia."

"PTSD?"

She nodded. "Among other things."

Somalia, with its war lords and lawlessness. She'd been facing those thugs? Chad pinched the bridge of his nose. Too many scenarios flashed through his mind. Too many questions. Troy had said Colombia had been a hell of a firefight; where else had she been? "Were you in charge of the op that went bad? Is that why he's after you?"

"No, I was in charge of his next mission. He wigged out and damned near caused us all to be killed. When we got back Cooper put him on administrative leave. Because I was the one who signed the report, he's focused on me as being the cause of all his problems."

"A variation of the 'kill the messenger' response." He'd seen it before. "Was Weir part of the decision making process?"

"No. Ed was part of the team, but I'm the only one he's targeting."

"I wouldn't be so sure about that." There was no way to break it to her gently, and no time either. "Weir's dead, Lauren."

Beside him, Troy swore and turned away. Lauren said nothing but color drained from her face.

"He was found this morning in a seedy hotel room up near Fredrick. According to the news reports, other guests reported hearing an argument in the middle of the night and called the front desk. When the police arrived, the room had been trashed and Weir was dead. His throat had been slit."

He narrowed his eyes at Lauren's curse.

He shared a confused look with Troy when she knelt at the side of the bed and stuck her hand between the box spring and mattress. "Lauren? What are you looking for?"

"The transponder."

"The what?" He took a step forward at the same time as Troy.

"A transponder—Ed gave it to me in case things went bad here and I needed to be extracted."

"You didn't have any sort of device with you." Troy's eyes were wide with horror when he met Chad's glance. "I swear, we checked. Walters went over her with a wand before they took off the first time, and we checked again right after I met her. We took her purse away, everything. There were no devices on her. I swear."

Lauren sat back on her heels and stared at the device she'd retrieved. It was smaller than the key fob Chad used to unlock his car doors. "Ed tucked it in my hair just before he left. Andy was thorough but you..."

"Just checked your fucking clothes," Troy snarled.

From the look on Troy's face, Chad was pretty sure if he hadn't been in the room Troy might have attacked Lauren.

Her fingers closed around the device. "Don't worry, it doesn't broadcast its location unless it's turned on. Which it hasn't been since I arrived. So if Harris took the other unit from Ed, he can't find me." She placed it on the floor. "We have to destroy this one so there's no chance it can ever broadcast our location. Troy, stomp on it. Break the damned thing."

"No. Don't," Chad barked when Troy took a step forward. "We might be able to use it to draw Harris in."

It was almost comical the way both Troy's and Lauren's expression mirrored identical looks of understanding within a split second of each other.

"We set him up." Troy scooped up the transponder and started pacing, toying with it with each step. "We choose a place we can watch without him realizing it. Make him think Lauren's there. Catch him in the act of breaking in."

"There's always the chance he may not have Ed's device or the right codes," Lauren said.

Chad shook his head. "Someone's going to know if it's among Weir's things. Sam said there was a single report on the news this morning but nothing since. Someone is keeping a lid on it." Which meant Davis had a helluva lot of connections to keep the press muzzled.

"Andy might be able to find out if it's missing through his police buddies," Troy suggested. "In the meantime, I'll take this effin' thing back to D.C. and set something up with Cooper so he can...*neutralize* Harris nice and quiet."

"We'll be fine with Andy in charge of things up here." Chad stopped Troy before he could leave the room. "When I came in, you two were talking about the club being used as a front. Lauren, will Harris be looking for you there?"

Lauren hesitated. "I don't think Harris knew anything about the club. There was some emergency going on that Cooper couldn't get away from, so he had Ed and I meet him there. It was one time only. I don't think any of the other team members knew about it, or would connect it with the group."

It didn't quite add up. If it was only used the one time, why refer to it as a front? "Tell me no one in the club has ever been put into any sort of danger."

"No." But doubt fluttered about the edges of her response. Shit, he had to get word out. Make sure Thalia stayed away. Sam and Rosie too.

"Is it possible Harris will go after Cooper himself?"

Lauren pursed her lips for a second before shaking her head. "Cooper's deliberately created opportunities for Harris to go after him if he wanted. As far as we can tell, Harris is fixated on me."

"Have you told me everything I should know about it?"

There was a split second's hesitation to her "yes" this time. Shit. Shit. SHIT.

"I've told you everything I'm *allowed* to tell you," she finally allowed.

His suspicions settled down at her answer. Somewhat. Rules and secrets were part of his world. And hers. “Is there anything you’re not telling me that might affect how we’ve set up the protection of this place? Or of the club?”

“No.” No hesitation.

All right, he could live with that. As long as she was telling him the truth. “When this is over, you and I are going to sit down and have a long talk.”

Troy snorted. “Since you’re both stuck here until we stop Harris, I’d say you two could start talking now.”

He turned on Troy. “Before you start casting stones, you might want to remember that you’ve known about this for almost a year and not said anything. So don’t go postal on Lauren for keeping quiet.”

Troy had the good grace to look away.

Chad rolled his shoulders, releasing the tension that had been building in them. “All right. Let’s plan what we’re going to do to draw him in. The sooner we can get it underway the sooner we can get out of here.”

Chapter Twelve

Lauren shifted her weight between the balls of her feet, watching for an opening. When she saw it, she brought up her knee and snapped her foot out, aiming toward Chad's solar plexus. Perhaps she'd telegraphed what she was going to do, or maybe she shouldn't have tried it twice in a row because this time he deflected the kick and spun away.

"You always did have a nice roundhouse."

"Thanks." She raised her hands and started circling again, allowing herself to admire the play of his shoulder muscles. Muscles that had rippled beneath her fingers the night before. The quick jab she took at him didn't make it past his glove.

For the next two minutes there was only the smack of leather on leather, and the occasional grunt when a hit connected, interrupting the silence of the gym. Then Chad telegraphed what she thought was going to be a right cross. Turned out it was a feint and he landed a forward kick to her solar plexus. She would have cursed him. If she could have drawn a breath.

"Shit! I tried to pull it but you leaned in." He grabbed her under her arms and held her so her lungs could fill with the air he'd knocked from her.

She hauled in a breath, then another. "Good one."

"Thanks."

Covered in sweat from her workout, Lauren stripped as she followed Chad to the bathroom. "Mind if I join you?"

The dark look he gave her sent a thrill down her spine and into her very core. "I'd be disappointed if you didn't."

He turned on the shower then stripped off his tee. Lauren frowned when he folded it before putting it in the hamper. She'd noticed that about him before—from the way his clothes were arranged in his closet, to how everything on his desk was neat and tidy. Even tidier than hers. "What's up with the neat freak routine all of a sudden? Did you have a housekeeper who complained about how you left your clothes on the floor the way you did when we were married?"

The heat in his eyes changed to ice, as did his tone. "There's no pleasing you, is there? When we were married, you'd complain that you were always having to pick up after me, and now I put things away properly, you're questioning me?"

Tread carefully. "I just wondered what changed—you never used to worry about dropping your clothes on the floor or leaving papers piled up on the desk..."

"What changed?" He advanced on her until they were inches apart. "You left. That's what changed."

Oh God. He didn't mean..."You thought if you kept things cleaner, if you hung up your clothes, I'd come back?" She reached up and stroked his neck. "Chad, I didn't leave you because you left your clothes on the floor. You know that, don't you?"

He shook his head. "All I knew was you weren't there anymore." He rested his forehead against hers. "I knew you were upset that I didn't talk to you about going against orders to protect Thalia but I couldn't go back into the past and change it."

"So you changed what you could." She wrapped her arms around him and laid her head on his shoulder. He stayed tense for a moment then relaxed and held her too. "We were both trying to change things in our own way, weren't we? To fix things we couldn't fix."

"I was willing to do anything I could to get you back."

She knew that feeling. After all, she'd spent years running, fixing up other people's messes, living from a suitcase while leaving no traces of herself wherever she went. How she wished there was some magic time machine...but there wasn't. "I know we can't go back, but is there a future for us?"

When this is over, will I lose you again?

His brows drew together in that familiar way.

"We have a lot to work out. I know there are things you're still not telling me."

She dropped her gaze. "You know I signed—"

"I'm not talking about your agreement with the Brigade. There's something else you're not telling me, isn't there? Like the divorce that you think I asked you for while I think it was the other way around. About the letters that you sent me that I never got."

"There are going to be some things you may not want to hear. I need you to trust me about some of the rest. That there may be things that I'm protecting you from."

"Did you remarry? Has there been someone else?"

She smiled at his gruff tone. He was jealous. "No. There's never been anyone else."

He fell silent for a moment but she didn't dare break the spell. "Remember I said I bought a house? I've spent a lot of time fixing it up—I've put in hardwood floors and torn out a lot of '70s paneling. I put in a new kitchen too."

She knew that already. Except Thalia had told her he'd bought it with his new wife. "I'd like to see it one day."

"You don't have to share a bedroom with me, but I've got one to spare. If you'd like."

That would last for...a minute. "I'd like that."

Footsteps slapped across the mats, slowed then stopped at the door. A half-second later, someone knocked. "You two decent in there?"

"Come on in."

Andy stuck his head in, his gaze taking a long sweep down Lauren's form that had a growl forming in Chad's throat.

"What do you want?"

"Troy called. The setup worked. They caught Harris attempting to break into the decoy home. He ate a bullet rather than be arrested." He tossed Lauren's cellphone to them; Chad caught it handily. "He says Lauren's boss wants to talk to you both."

Chapter Thirteen

Lauren pulled the Brigade's Humvee into the driveway of a modest two-story Colonial Chad had directed her to. It was the type they used to drive by and say *some day, we'll own a house like that.* A massive beech tree shaded the front lawn, though its leaves now covered the lawn not the branches. She could picture Chad playing catch with a son, or daughter, beneath it. Or maybe he'd put up a hoop over the two-car garage and teach their child how to free throw. If she even dared thinking about having another child.

One hurdle at a time.

"You're right. It's just the type of house we used to dream about." She pulled the keys from the ignition and pressed the button to release the trunk latch.

"I'll get it," he said calmly when she reached for the door handle.

Ever the gentleman, he walked around the car and held open the door for her. She took the hand he offered to help her out—it wasn't that she needed the help. Or maybe, from the way her knees were shaking, she did.

Lauren tightened the grip on her purse and followed him in, waiting in the open doorway while he turned off the alarm. A beam of late afternoon sunlight bounced off the crystal chandelier hanging from the two-story ceiling. The oak banister gleamed as if it had just been polished, as did the matching hardwood floor. "It's beautiful."

"Do you want a tour?" Chad had his hands stuck in his pockets again, a sign she remembered meant he was nervous. At least she wasn't the only one whose knees were beating a tattoo to rival a woodpecker.

She trailed him as he took her on a tour of the house. They started in the kitchen where she admired the glass-fronted units and granite counter then proceeded through the first floor—an office they could share, the living room with its marble-fronted fireplace and two-story wood-beamed ceilings.

"I hired an architect to redesign it," he explained when they reached the top floor. "It used to be a four bedroom but I had him combine one of the smaller bedrooms with the master. You'd always said you wanted an ensuite...I thought maybe..."

That if he'd made everything perfect, she'd come back to him. The same way he'd become almost obsessive about picking up his clothes and keeping things neat. "Show me?"

He held out his hand, waiting until she'd laced their fingers together before leading her to the master suite dominated by a king-sized bed.

"I can't tell you how long I've waited to show you this room. To..." He shook his head. "Never mind. One day at a time, right?"

Right about certain things. But not for what she sensed he needed. "To what? To make love to me? To tie me up and have your way with me the way we used to?"

"Yes." Need and desire filled both his voice and his eyes.

"So what are you waiting for? I'm here. Tell me what you want me to do."

"Take your clothes off." A command, not a question. A

shiver of anticipation ran up her spine with heated fingers.

Dropping her purse on the floor, she removed her holster and placed it on the dresser. She slipped off her blouse, then unhooked her bra and let it fall beside her purse. Her slacks hit the floor moments later followed by her thin, lacy boy shorts. Her pulse jacked into the triple digits as she stood naked while he was completely clothed. The air in the room thinned and heated at the same time, especially as his gaze raked her.

"Play with yourself. Touch yourself the way you want me to touch you." His voice rasped over her skin, setting her nerve endings on fire as if he'd scraped her all over with sandpaper.

The way she wanted him to touch her? She let her head fall back and closed her eyes as she fondled her breasts. As she had so many times in the past, she imagined it was his fingers stroking the sensitive skin, tweaking her nipples.

"Don't close your eyes, Lauren. Look at me while you're pleasuring yourself."

Her eyelids were heavy but she forced them open and found he'd moved closer. She pinched her nipples hard enough to create a sting that soon changed to heat. *This, this is what I want you to do.* She tugged and rolled them again and again, the moisture below gathering as the sensation shot to her pussy.

Not breaking her gaze, one hand slipped over her belly and between her thighs. Cream drenched her fingers as they slid through her folds.

"Is that what you want me to do to you?"

"Yes."

He crowded her, so close the heat from his body warmed her over-sensitized skin. "My mouth or my fingers?"

"Either. Both." While her one hand continued to play with

her breasts, her hips rotated, pressing her clit against her palm. She quickened her pace then needing more, plunged one finger, then another inside her. Each breath grew harder to draw. "Oh God, Chad, I want you inside me. Your fingers, your cock, I don't care. I need..."

Before she could push herself over the edge and climax, Chad grabbed her hand from between her legs. He lifted it to his mouth, sucking first one finger then the other. Once they were clean, he bent his head and captured one of her taut nipples with his teeth while his other hand ventured where hers had been.

Lauren moaned as he plunged his fingers inside her at the same time he nipped at her breast. The stinging caused by his teeth combined with the pleasure of his fingers until she had to hang onto his shoulders to remain upright. He varied the speed and the depth of his penetration, bringing her close to climax at least twice before he withdrew.

As much as she wanted to moan her complaint, to beg him to let her come, she kept her mouth shut. He took great pride in making her come multiple times, so whatever he had planned, she was prepared to wait him out.

"Kneel on the bed with your ass in the air."

She did as he bid, turning her head to watch him methodically strip. He removed his gun from its holster and placed it in the bedside table. Leaving her waiting was part of his plan she decided as he opened the closet and hung his suit jacket. Like at the farm, he folded his shirt and placed it in the hamper. She used the time to watch the play of muscles on his back and abdomen as he stripped his trousers and hung them on a press. When he was finally naked, his cock was still fully erect. Instead of returning to her, he headed into the bathroom.

She didn't have to ask what he was looking for—she'd

known as soon as he'd turned her onto her stomach what he'd want. He returned a few moments later, his erection hard and tall against his belly.

Her eyes widened at the items he carried upon his return. The butt plug he placed on the mattress beside her was at least the same size as his cock so she wasn't too worried about it, but her pulse raced at the riding crop he set beside her.

He knelt behind her and murmured, "Spread your legs wider, babe."

She shuffled until her knees were the distance apart he'd indicated. As soon as she stopped moving, he picked up the bottle of lube and applied a generous dollop to the anal plug and coated it with his fingers. "Relax."

It was easier for him to say than for her to do, especially when he squirted lube over her behind. And even tougher when he pressed the hard tip of the plug against her opening. As he pressed it inward, his other hand toyed with her clit. Before she knew it, her hips were rotating against his fingers, her ass pressed against the plug and it popped past the ring of muscles. "Stand up, Lauren."

She carefully pushed herself to a stand. His features, normally so carefully controlled, were unguarded, the lust and desire filling his eyes, hardening his lips. He wanted her like this. He needed her. As much as she needed him.

She stayed still as he fixed the harness to the plug and around her hips.

"Get back on the bed the way you were before. Grab hold of the headboard."

She bit her lip to keep herself from moaning and hurried to position herself the way he'd ordered. He'd not fastened the second cuff around her wrist securing her to the headboard, and she was already trembling in anticipation.

After laying a kiss on her shoulder, he set to work massaging her shoulders and working down her back with the skill of a trained masseuse. By the time he'd reached her hips, she'd forgotten about the restraints. Hell, her body had forgotten it had bones, she was so relaxed. If she'd been a cat, she'd have been purring.

He shifted his weight, parting her legs so he could kneel between them. His fingers trailed over the globes of her cheeks and down to her pussy. She just about purred when he dipped them into her opening and filled her. Between his thumb on her clit and his two fingers deep inside, he soon had her pressing back, her body heating as her second orgasm overtook her.

Until he picked up the riding crop she'd forgotten. He'd spanked her on occasion, a light tap on her behind, and she'd enjoyed it, but this...this was different. This would hurt.

He leaned over her, stroking the leather strip of the crop down her spine. Her body tensed, tightening around the butt plug until it felt massive.

"You either trust me." His fingers parted her folds and unerringly found her clit, toying with it until she was ready to agree to anything. Then he withdrew. "Or you don't."

If he'd wanted to seek revenge from her, wouldn't he have done that back at the farm?

"Lauren?"

You either trust me or you don't. It was a test. She closed her eyes and nodded. "I trust you, Chad."

She'd barely finished speaking when the crop whistled across her left butt cheek. A second stroke followed the first, this one over the right buttock. While it initially stung, it didn't hurt. He struck each cheek twice more, then smoothed the sting with his hand. Once she realized it wouldn't hurt, he continued until her ass was on fire and her pussy dripped with her arousal.

He settled beneath her thighs, using his tongue on her clit, his fingers scissoring into her tight passage. Alternating between licking her clit and tugging on it with his lips, he took her to the brink of orgasm. She couldn't stop herself from crying out when he let her fly, her body clenching around his fingers and the plug, pulsing in ecstasy.

Her pussy hadn't stopped pulsing when he withdrew the plug leaving her feeling emptier than she could ever remember. Without giving her any warning, he thrust in hard, stretching her, the burning pain mixing with an unending pleasure of the remains of her last orgasm. Only he'd known what she liked, how she liked.

He tangled his fingers in her hair, pulling it until her head arched back. He withdrew and slammed back in again until she shuddered around him. "Do you feel how much I want you?"

"Yessss..." As much as she wanted him.

"Do you know I've never taken another woman here? That I've never wanted to?"

Realizing it was important to him, she found the breath to speak. "No one else has been there either."

At her confession, he slowed his thrusts with a groan. Moving ever so slowly he withdrew then returned.

She pressed her hips back against him, tightening her muscles, holding him in. His fingers dug into her hips as he gave into the pleasure. When he began a series of frenzied thrusts that pushed her closer and closer to the edge of her third orgasm, she buried her face in the sheets. God, how bland the last decade had been without the fire he'd brought to her, the strength of her orgasm rippled through her.

Moments later, Chad's cock pulsed deep inside her, his come heating her passage until every inch of her felt aflame.

The sensation paled to the heat of his breath on her shoulder or his gasped "love you".

As soon as he fell on the mattress beside her, Lauren attempted to roll to him, to hold him only to be stopped by the bonds holding her in place.

Still breathing heavily, Chad cracked open an eye at her curses. "Hang on a sec."

He reached up and loosened the bindings, but not before he'd taken her breath away again with another deep kiss. Once she was free, he gathered her in his arms. Lauren would have been content to lie there for the rest of the night, to hold him and be held. Instead Chad slipped a hand beneath her knees and lifted her. "Come on, let's get cleaned up."

The ensuite bathroom he'd had designed was a work of art. Where he'd taken charge in the bedroom, she pressed him against the tiles and picked up a bar of soap. The room filled with steam from the multiple showerheads and the occasional soft murmur as they cleaned up. They both seemed to sense there was no need for words, simply being in the same room together again was enough. The last of the lather swirling down the drain, Lauren wrapped her arms around Chad's waist and rested her head on his shoulder. "I love you too."

His "hmm" of satisfaction turned into a chuckle when her stomach growled loudly enough to be heard over the water. "Do you want to go out for dinner tonight or order in?"

"In." Preferably something they could eat while sprawled naked on the bed.

He grabbed a towel from the rack and wrapped it around her, and tucked the end into her cleavage. Before he could wrap his towel around his hip, Lauren took it from him. She lingered over her task, patting every single part of him dry. The sun had long since set when they finally walked back into the bedroom.

Chad flicked on the light. Before she could step around him, he'd shoved her behind him but she hit the doorframe with an oomph.

"Stay where you are, Mr. Miller." Shit, there was a man in their bedroom.

Chad held out his hands and adopted the reasonable tone they'd been taught during their hostage negotiation training at Quantico. "Tom? Put the gun down and let's talk about what you're doing here."

Gun. Her empty holster lay on the bed. Aw fuck. It was her own gun that Tom Whoever was using.

"I don't think so. I know you're hiding a whore behind you. You tell her to come out where I can see her." Lauren didn't recognize the voice, but being called a whore had her balling her fists.

"Tom, the woman behind me isn't a whore. It's my wife. You remember Lauren, don't you?"

It was someone they knew? Lauren peered over his shoulder. It startled her to recognize their intruder. The man she'd last seen as a fourteen-year-old boy now stood at least two inches taller than Chad. "Tommy Jenkins?"

"What are you doing here, Mrs. Miller?" From the way her Sig Sauer shook he was likely to shoot one of them accidentally. "You shouldn't be here."

His gaze dropped to the bed, his forehead wrinkling. "You guys had sex? Didn't you?" The gun steadied and returned to point at Chad. "Did you rape her? The way you did last time?"

"He's never raped me!" Lauren couldn't stop her response.

"Yes, he has. I saw it." Tom used both hands to steady his grip. The shaking stopped only marginally. "It was on all the websites, on all the news reports. He'd tied you up and blindfolded you. He made you," his voice dropped to a whisper, "do things. Bad things."

"Chad never raped me," she repeated, keeping her voice steady. How the hell could she get him to understand that she'd asked Chad to do that to her? That she enjoyed being bound and blindfolded. "He's never hurt me, Tommy. I promise."

"You're just saying that to protect him. You shouldn't do that. He's a bad man. You need to stay away from him. You hate him, remember? He killed your baby. He killed Emily."

"No. No, he didn't." She sidled away from Chad, attempting to draw Tom's attention away so Chad could get to the drawer where he'd stashed his gun. If they were lucky, Tom hadn't already found it.

She took another step toward him but also to the left, drawing his attention further away from Chad. "Chad didn't kill Emily. Neither of us did." She took a deep breath but didn't dare close her eyes the way she wanted. "She just stopped breathing. There was nothing either of us could have done."

"No! He killed her." With a roar of anger, Tom swung the gun back toward Chad, who dived to the floor at the same time the gun went off.

Chapter Fourteen

Pain seared Chad's shoulder like someone had stabbed him with a red-hot poker. Even as he fell, he saw Lauren kicked Tom in the back of the knees and grapple for the gun.

His right arm not working properly, Chad dragged himself across the floor, the six feet between him and his weapon a chasm wider than the Grand Canyon. Using his left hand, he opened the drawer and felt around inside until his fingers closed around the barrel of his Glock. He rolled over just in time to see Lauren's head snap back. Blood spurted across the room, splattering over the sheets. Lauren's body toppled sideways.

FUCK! Chad aimed his gun but Tom dragged Lauren to her feet and used her as a shield. "Stay back! I didn't want to hurt her but I had to. You saw—she was fighting me."

Lauren's head lolled onto her chest and he couldn't see her face properly, but from the blood trailing down her shirt, the bastard had probably broken her nose. Hopefully that's all he'd done. "Set her down, Tom. Please. Let me look after her. Let me make sure she's all right."

"Uh uh." Tom shifted Lauren's dead weight to one arm and lifted the gun, aiming it at Chad. He tilted his head until his mouth was less than an inch away from Lauren's ear, but his gaze never left Chad. "You shouldn't have come back, Mrs. Miller. You should have stayed away. He was miserable when you left. I was sad too but I knew you were safe."

Chad held his own gun steady but couldn't fire without risking Lauren's life. At least the gun was aimed at him, not at Lauren's head. Though the rest of Lauren didn't move, the fingers on Lauren's right hand made the "OK" sign. It was all he could do not to heave a sigh of relief. She was all right. If they kept their heads, if he could get control of this situation, they could still get out of this. Maybe. Tom still had that fucking gun.

Tom's eyes went unfocused, dreamy, his voice soft and distant. The arm holding the gun dropped a few inches but not enough. If Chad moved now, he'd still be gut-shot. "I loved you so much, Mrs. Miller. You were such a good mother to Emily."

"She was; you're right." *Come on, Lauren, move. Drop to the floor. Something that'll get you out of the line of sight and give me a clean shot at him.*

Tom's gaze cleared and the black barrel of the gun stared at Chad again. From this distance, a two-fingered monkey couldn't miss hitting him. "Don't you talk to her. You're not good enough for her. That's why I had to keep her away from you. Keep her safe."

Chad held up the hand he could move, spreading his fingers wide. "All right. Let's just calm down."

"I kept her safe from you. I checked your mail box every day so you couldn't get any of the letters she sent you. I deleted all her messages from your answering machine. You didn't even know I was there. You thought you were so good with your security system. But you couldn't stop me."

Shit, he'd given Tom the security code and asked him to check his mail and water the plants when he was away. The whole time the little shit was the reason Lauren hadn't come home?

With a move so fast it startled even Chad who had been looking for a sign, Lauren dropped to the ground, taking Tom with her. As Tom swung around with a curse, aiming Lauren's own gun at her, Chad aimed and squeezed the trigger.

Chapter Fifteen

"They've charged Jenkins with attempted murder and aggravated assault." Sam glanced at Lauren as she settled onto the arm of the couch beside Chad. "He's lawyered up, and isn't talking, but from what Andy's been able to find out through his sources his lawyers are seeking a psychiatric review while he's still in the hospital."

"They're looking for an insanity plea," Lauren surmised. "Or at least diminished capacity."

"They'll get it." Chad covered her knee with his left hand. His right was bound to his side, the bandage where they'd operated on the bullet not as thick as it had been the day before.

"What I don't get is why he waited this long to go after Chad."

"I talked to his mom." The petite woman who Chad had introduced as Rosalinda Ramos, Sam's fiancée answered Lauren's question. "She said he'd had a breakdown at school, enough that the counselors there suggested he come home for the semester."

Sam scowled. "Except he came home and found his mom with a black eye." He held up a hand when Chad cursed under his breath. "Don't worry, her rat-bastard ex didn't give it to her this time. I checked. Patsy had been in a car accident and she got it from that. She's fine, by the way."

"We're guessing that he saw the article in the Post on the weekend and that made him want to check up on you."

"From there," Sam picked up where Rosie left off, "we're not sure if it was seeing you two together again that set him off. Or if he'd planned to go after Chad all along."

Lauren suppressed a smile. The duo were completing each other's sentences as if they'd been married for years.

"Almost forgot. Hey, Rosebud, you got those photocopies?"

Rosie reached into a voluminous purse and pulled out a manila file folder. "The police found these when they went through Tom's apartment. I got Andy to use his connections to make some copies since they have to keep the originals as evidence."

Lauren took the folder and handed it to Chad who placed it on his lap and opened it. Her breath caught in her throat when she recognized her own handwriting. "My letters."

After a glance at her, Sam nodded and returned his attention to Chad. "Looks like Tom had been going through your mail for years."

"I'd asked him to pick it up for me whenever I was travelling. I had no idea he'd been holding things back."

The room was silent except for the sound of rustling paper as Chad flipped through the letters. He stopped at the final one, written two years after she'd left. The one pleading with him to phone her, to give her some sign that he'd give her another chance.

He stared up at her, his heart in his eyes. "I'm sorry, babe. I would have replied if I'd known."

"It wasn't your fault." She covered his hand with hers and squeezed it. "But we've got a second chance now."

Sam stood, holding a hand out to help Rosie to her feet. “Well, Rosebud, I think that’s our cue to leave these two alone.”

Leaving Chad to rest on the couch, Lauren showed them to the front door. “Sam, I owe you an apology. I know I blamed you for Jill’s death all these years. I was wrong. I’m sorry.”

He quirked his eyebrows up. “I know. I’d say we both owe each other some apologies. I’ve been blaming you for walkin’ out on Chad. I had no idea why you’d gone or what you were going through. If I’d known...” He nodded. “Yeah, we both had our demons to fight, didn’t we?”

“So...are we friends again?”

“Yup.” He grinned. “I heard you quit your other job. If you ever feel the itch to get back in the field, I know a good firm that’s lookin’ for people with your background.”

“I may just take you up on that offer.” Once she’d figured out the rest of her life.

“You do that.” His grin faded and his gaze drifted to the room behind her. “It damned near killed him when you left. He stopped going home, started sleeping in the office for months at a time. I was afraid I was going to come in one day and find he’d eaten his gun.”

“I didn’t know. I thought...I got some bad intel and thought he’d remarried within a year.”

“Mmm. Now I wonder where you heard that?” One dark eyebrow arched up, but when she didn’t answer, Sam sighed. “Don’t leave him again without telling him exactly why, you hear? Don’t disappear the way you did last time. Or I’ll come after you.”

Without waiting for a reply, he headed for his car. Lauren stood in the doorway, until the Jag disappeared from sight.

Once she’d shut the door and rearmed the security system,

Lauren returned to find Chad with his head against the back of the couch, his eyes closed. "You should go upstairs and have a nap."

He roused and smiled at her. The look he gave her was all heat. "You coming up with me?"

"Men! Even hurt and exhausted, all you can think about is sex." She folded her arms over her chest and tried not to smile. And failed.

"The problem with that is...?"

"As tempting as your offer is, if I lie down with you, you'll do anything but nap." She helped him to his feet and followed him upstairs.

Once they got to the bedroom, he started to undo his shirt left-handed. "Damn it, I'm all thumbs."

"Here, let me." She flicked open the buttons of his shirt, loving the familiarity of the task. Her smile dimmed when she caught sight of the bandage over his shoulder. It was smaller than the one the doctors had originally placed there, but it still looked obscene.

Chad rested his forehead on hers. "Hey, it'll heal, babe. I'll be fine."

"I could have lost you again," she whispered. "I shouldn't have left my gun out in plain sight. I should have locked it up so he couldn't get it."

"And I should have remembered to re-arm the security system so we would have had a warning. Hell, I should have locked the front door, but I had other things on my mind and I let myself get distracted." He stroked his thumb over her nipple until it beaded. "Stop blaming yourself. It's over. Harris is dead, and Tom's not a threat anymore either. We've got a second chance, babe. Let's not waste it."

"You're right," she decided.

"Of course I am. Now why don't you get undressed and join me? I'll let you be on top."

She had to laugh at the exaggerated leer he gave her. "You're incorrigible. All right, I'll lie down with you, but we're not going to do anything more than sleep."

She hovered over him while he took his pain pills and lay on the bed with him. Within five minutes, he was asleep and she found herself staring at the ceiling. Two weeks ago she'd only dreamt that she'd be lying here beside Chad again, and now her dreams had come true.

Yet there were still so many things unsettled between them.

Chad rolled over, his arm instinctively seeking Lauren only to find...nothing. "Lauren?"

Had it all been a dream? He opened his eyes. The dent her head had left in the pillow was still there, the side of her bed messed. No, it hadn't been a dream. So why wasn't she still here?

Maybe she'd gone to the bathroom? Nope, the door was open and the light off. Where the hell had she gone?

His heart clogging his throat, he jogged downstairs, half afraid he'd find her bags missing. He pulled up short when he heard her talking in the kitchen.

"I meant what I said, Coop. I'm not coming back. I'm through with the Brigade."

Cooper was here? What the hell else did that bastard want? He'd already visited Chad at the hospital and threatened him until he'd signed a secrecy agreement similar to the one that bound Lauren.

"No, I haven't and I'm not going to either." There was a

pause which told him that Cooper wasn't there in person, Lauren was talking to him on the phone. "No, you can't talk to him. He's sleeping...No, I am not waking him up so you can talk to him. He just got out of the hospital, damn it."

He was half-tempted to go into the kitchen and tell Cooper to go stuff himself, but he enjoyed hearing Lauren defend him. Other than Sam, he'd had precious few people in his corner. Besides, if he showed her he was awake, she'd probably insist on making him lunch—dinner, he revised having a glance at the chiming clock on the wall. He'd slept longer than he thought. While he was hungry, he preferred for her to come upstairs to wake him so he could make a meal of her.

He headed back to the stairs then saw the file folder containing the photocopies of Lauren's letters. Maybe he should read them before they made any long term decisions. He tucked the folder under his arm and headed back to the bedroom. Once he was stretched out on the bed, he steeled himself and opened the folder. From the looks of it, Sam had arranged the letters by the date they'd been sent.

April 26, 2002

Dear Chad,

I know you don't understand why I left without talking to you, but I was afraid of what I might do if I didn't get help right away. I've tried to be strong for you, but I just couldn't get my head clear. I've checked myself into a private hospital under an assumed name so the reporters can't attack you because of me...

The rest of the letter explained about Tranquil Pastures, and her diagnosis, just as she'd said. She'd pleaded with him to phone her or write her back.

May 11, 2002

...I love you, Chad. I'm so sorry for what I said during that fight. I know Emily didn't die because of anything you did. It was my fault, all mine, and I cannot beg your forgiveness enough...

The second letter continued, with yet another plea for him to write if he couldn't phone, to let her know he was all right, and asked if he'd consider visiting her until she was well enough to come home. So did the third. And the fourth.

The fifth letter wasn't written by Lauren but by her psychiatrist.

Dear Mr. Miller,

It is vital to your wife's recovery...

Chad crumpled the letter in his fist. Damn Tom Jenkins. Lauren had needed him.

Dear Chad, He checked the date, this had been written six months after her first letter. *I've been praying that you'd get in contact with me after Dr. Maudsley wrote to you. Since we haven't heard from you, I can only assume you don't want me to come home to live with you when I'm released the day after tomorrow...*

He closed his eyes. *I would have come for you if I'd known, babe. Nothing could have stopped me.*

February 13, 2004

Dear Chad,

I received the divorce papers from your attorney today. I had hoped that perhaps we could work on repairing our marriage, but Thalia tells me that you've been dating someone else for the past few months and that the two of you have moved in together. I hope she is stronger for you than I have been, and that she makes you happy because you deserve happiness. I will always regret that I couldn't be the one to give it to you. I love you, and always will...

He had to read the last line twice, then re-read the paragraph again. *Thalia* had told Lauren he was living with someone? Lauren had said once that she'd heard he was living with someone, but not once could he remember her saying that it was his own sister who had lied to her.

His BlackBerry rang. A quick check of the caller ID had him answering. "I was wondering how long it would take before you called, Coop."

"Lauren said you were asleep."

"I was." *Yet you called me anyway. Arrogant ass.*

Cooper grunted, which would be as close to an apology as he'd get Chad supposed. "I heard Sam came to visit you earlier."

"You heard or are you having us watched?"

"I ran into him and Rosie at the club, and he mentioned he'd dropped by. I thought I'd better make sure you completely understand that agreement you signed yesterday means you can't tell him anything about what you've learned."

Since I was still half doped up when you made me sign that fucking paper, you mean.

"I haven't said a word to him or anyone else." Yet. "I want your assurance you will never use the club for anything related to the Brigade ever again. Because if I ever find you have put anyone at that club in danger, I am coming after you."

"Just make sure you keep your mouth shut to Sam. And anyone else."

"Considering you threatened to take me into custody if I didn't, I don't have much of a choice, do I? Are we done?"

"No. I want you to convince Lauren to come back and work for the Brigade. She doesn't have to go back into the field, but I need her."

Tough shit. So did he. So had he for the last ten years.

"That's not my decision to make, Coop. It's hers. If she wants to come back, I won't stand in her way, but if she doesn't, I'll support her a hundred and ten percent."

"Hmm, I'll remember you said that if you decide things won't work between you." Cooper's voice was cool, almost threatening.

"Whether we stay together or not, I'll still support her."

"Good to hear." To his surprise, Cooper sounded approving. "By the way, I know Lauren doesn't believe me but if I'd known what Thalia had done back then I would have told Thal to back off and made sure Lauren came home."

"Thalia? What the—" Cooper had already cut the connection and Chad found himself talking to no one.

Just what the fuck had Thalia done?

Chapter Sixteen

Lauren opened the French doors and stepped onto the gray patio stones, the only ornament in the back garden. While Chad might have worked wonders inside the house, the yard had been left virtually untouched. In the spring, she'd plant daisies and black-eyed susans along the back fence. Maybe some sunflowers, and a rose trellis beside the patio so the fragrance could waft in when the door was open. And a fountain would be nice. One the birds could dart into and drink from or bathe in. There's always been something soothing about listening to trickling water in the lazy summer days.

If she still lived here next summer.

Chad had changed. So had she. Not for the worse. They were just...different. Subtle changes they'd both have to adjust to, accept. Yet so much about them was the same. He could still read her moods, still knew what she found exciting in the bedroom and knew the exact amount of force to set her on fire. But a marriage couldn't be built only on what happened in the bedroom.

The doorbell chimed, rousing her from her musings. After diverting to the kitchen to place her cup in the sink, she checked the monitor installed over the front door.

Thalia. Shit. She'd hoped it would be a couple more days before she'd face her again. Maybe she could just not answer the door. Pretend they weren't here.

After a gesture from her sister-in-law, Thalia's husband pressed the doorbell again. Damn it, they were going to wake Chad up if she didn't answer it.

Cursing under her breath, Lauren turned off the alarm and flipped the deadbolt. Steeling herself, she opened the door. "Hello, Thalia."

Thalia hissed and her eyes narrowed when she recognized who had opened the door. "What the hell are you doing here, Lauren? You're supposed to be in Europe."

"Nice to see you too. What do you want?"

"I heard that my brother had been shot. I came to see if he needed any help."

While Lauren couldn't fault Chad's sister for worrying about Chad, she resented the unspoken implication that she was incapable of caring for him. "He's fine. He may have to do some physio for a couple months, but he'll recover."

Ignoring her husband behind her, Thalia rolled her chair to the door. "I want to see him."

For the first time, Lauren realized the step had been designed as a ramp. As much as she wanted to leave Thalia on the doorstop and close the door between them, Chad would never appreciate her treating his sister that way. She sighed and opened the door all the way. "I really wish you'd come back another time. He's sleeping right now."

"Good." Thalia rounded on her. "I thought we had an agreement that you were to stay away from my brother. Permanently."

"You lied, Thalia. Repeatedly. That voided any agreement as far as I was concerned."

"You weren't right for him. I couldn't let you get back

together so I did what I had to do to protect him."

"I love Chad, Thal. I always did, and I always will."

"You signed the divorce agreement quickly enough," Thalia sneered.

"Only because you told me he wanted to get married again. If I'd come back when I wanted to, we might have had a chance."

"He needed someone better than you. Someone stronger."

Lauren ran her hand through her hair. Ten years before, she'd have agreed. Now? Not a chance. "I trusted you, Thalia. I thought we were friends, but we weren't. Were we ever?"

"You were his wife—you were supposed to be on his side no matter what happened. You weren't there for him the way you should have been."

"I was there."

"No. You weren't. Not like me." Thalia rolled her chair forward, until Lauren was forced to step back. "You should have backed him a hundred percent for having the guts to go against orders to protect me. Instead you questioned him, argued with him about it. When that video got out, you should have held up your head and proudly admitted you submitted to him. That he was your Dominant. Yet you didn't."

The video. She'd often wondered how the press had managed to get a video camera into their bedroom. "You did that, didn't you? You placed the camera in our bedroom."

"It had to be done."

"Why? Goddamn it, Thalia, why?" she shouted. "Why would you do that to us? Violate our privacy like that?"

"Because you didn't agree with Chad about his decision to protect me. To protect the club members. He saved my life with that decision, you selfish bitch," Thalia bit out. "If it had been up to you, I would have died. But all you could think about was your pitiful career."

"I understood why he felt he needed to protect you, but there were other ways to protect you. More official ways. I knew how much his career with the Bureau meant to him and he sacrificed it for you." Lauren's nails dug into her palms. "If he'd come to me, we could have found some other way to help protect the club. It was his not telling me what he'd done that was the issue between us. That's why I felt betrayed, because he didn't come to me first."

"He didn't tell you because you were too busy blaming him and everyone else for Emily's death," Thalia snapped. "It was *your* fault my niece died. Your fault."

"No, it wasn't."

They both looked to the top of the stairs where Chad stood, his good hand on the bannister, his gaze locked on Lauren. How much had he heard?

Thalia lifted her chin as Chad walked down the stairs to join them, but Lauren didn't miss the way her throat moved, the way the vein in her neck pulsed. Her sister-in-law was nervous.

"I heard about what happened. About the shooting." Thalia rolled her chair forward. "I can move in here and care for you. I can bring some of my people over to help out. You don't need her here."

"Is Lauren right? Are you the one who put that video camera in our bedroom?"

Thalia looked away.

"You were, weren't you?" Chad's scowl deepened, his eyes grew dark as a thundercloud when he stopped in front of her. "Then you sent it to that goddamned gossip site who put it on the internet. Let it go viral."

"They had to see," she whispered. "*You* had to see her for what she was."

"What she was? She was my *wife*." He grabbed the armrest of her wheelchair and leaned until their noses were an inch apart. "You damned near irreparably damaged both of our reputations. You made it impossible for either of us to walk down the street without people making snide comments. If it hadn't been for Sam deciding to start Hauberk, I probably would have ended up a mall cop or asking a customer if they wanted fries with their order."

"I did what was necessary." Thalia's chin went down a half inch before she jerked it back up. "You need someone strong. Someone willing to get down on their knees and submit to you the way you deserved."

"That's your kink, not mine."

Lauren stifled her sigh when Thalia shook her head and persisted. "She's not good for you, Chad. Why am I the only one who can see that?"

"It's not your decision to make. It's mine." He moved to stand beside Lauren, slipped his arm around her waist. "I've asked Lauren to move back in with me. Whether we'll make it, I don't know yet, but hear me now: I will not tolerate any more interference. Because so help me God, Thal, if I find out you've been lying to me or withholding information or manipulating either of us ever again, I will cut you out of my life forever." Chad glanced at Spencer. "Take your wife home and don't bring her back unless you personally hear me invite her."

He waited until the door had closed behind the couple before he spoke again. "I had no idea it had been Thalia who brought the divorce agreement to you, or that she'd told you I was marrying someone else."

"I know." *Now.*

"Why didn't you tell me it was Thalia? Were you afraid I'd believe her over you?"

"No. To be honest, that never occurred to me."

"So these past few days, why not say 'Thalia lied to me'? Why did you keep referring to her as 'someone' or 'I heard'? Why protect her after what she'd done to you? To us?"

Wasn't it obvious? "Because she's your sister. I didn't want to come between you."

"And you're my wife but that didn't stop her from coming between us." He wrapped his good arm around her and tucked her head beneath his chin. "Between Thalia with her lies and her videotape, and Jenkins stealing your letters...it's enough to make you wonder if they were conspiring to keep us apart."

She snuggled closer, enjoying being back in his embrace. Now that Thalia's manipulations had been brought into the light, the lingering guilt of not telling Chad dissipated. She felt like she could fly. Or burst into song. Neither of which would be pretty. "Paranoia, party of two, your table's ready."

"Even paranoids have enemies." Chad steered her to the stairs. "Think about it, Lauren. If Thalia hadn't taken that video of us, Tom may not have taken the letters trying to save you from me. If I'd read even one of those, I would have hopped on a plane and gone after you and—"

She pulled back and placed a finger over his lips. "Sssh. You can drive yourself crazy thinking like that. We can't change what's already happened or what others do as much as we wish we could. We can only control our own actions."

He touched his lips to her hair. "I know, but they kept me from the most precious thing in my life. I'm not sure I'll ever be able to forgive them for that."

"Give yourself time." They had all the time in the world now and she planned on not wasting another second.

Neither of them spoke when she took his hand and led him upstairs and into the bedroom. No words were needed as they undressed each other. Or when their lips touched. Or when he lowered her onto the bed, rolling beneath her, letting her take charge just the way he'd promised earlier.

Taking care not to touch his shoulder, Lauren stretched over his body and reclaimed his mouth. The outside world disappeared until only the two of them existed, filled with their languid explorations of each other, with gentle touches and soft sighs. Time slowed and stretched as if they'd never been apart.

When she could hold off no longer, Lauren positioned herself over Chad and bore down, taking him into her body an inch at a time. They both exhaled when their hips touched. His eyes dark, Chad caressed her breast, touching her reverently, carefully, as if she might shatter. She met his gaze, quickly losing herself within his deep gray depths.

The desire and passion of the very first time they'd made love flooded Lauren's soul. It twined itself around her heart and held fast.

With a light touch to her back, he drew her down until one nipple hovered above his mouth. When his lips closed over the sensitive bud, the sensation streaked through her and down to her pussy as if she'd been struck by lightning. His hands smoothed over her belly, following its path, his fingers finding her clit, pleasuring her until she could stay still no longer.

Whenever she started to speed up, he slowed her down. He stroked and suckled and teased until her whole body was quivering, heated until she was sure she would spontaneously combust. A simple touch of his thumb to her clit triggered an orgasm that shattered her into a thousand pieces of pure sensation.

When she finally could breathe, he started all over again,

this time following her lead when her body clamped around him, milking his cock in the hardest orgasm she'd ever had.

Night had long since fallen before Chad finally spoke. "There's never been anyone else for me, Lauren."

He curled his fingers beneath her chin and turned her face until she looked at him. "I would have met you at the airport if I'd known you were waiting for my response. Hell, I should have flown to England to be with you as soon as I found out where you'd gone."

"You couldn't leave. Your inquiry was coming up."

"I didn't have to be there. They'd already made their judgment." He rested his forehead against hers. "I loved you, Lauren. I would have done anything to get you back."

"Loved, past tense?" she whispered.

"No. Love. Past, present and future."

The fear and doubt Thalia had long ago planted withered. They could do this, they could make their marriage work. "I love you, too."

"Past, present and future?" His voice was hoarse and his thumb shook as he wiped a tear from her cheek she hadn't realized had fallen.

Filled with hope that she hadn't had for years, she nodded. "I've never stopped loving you. I loved you then, I love you now. I'll love you forever."

About the Author

Growing up in rural Ontario with little else to amuse her, Leah Braemel created her own adventures by writing her own stories. In her teens, she discovered her love of romances. Soon all her stories revolved around giving her heroes and heroines their Happy-Ever-After.

Married to her college sweetheart and the mother of two sons, Leah is the only woman in a houseful of men—even their cat is male. After a conversation with her eldest son about how he needed to follow his dreams, Leah decided she needed to take her own advice and make her dreams of getting published come true. She was thrilled when her first sizzling romance, *Private Property*, was published by Samhain Publishing in 2009.

In 2010, the reviewers at The Romance Studio nominated *Private Property* for a CAPA award for Best Erotic Romance. Leah was also nominated in the Best Erotic Romance Author category. Reviewers have since awarded her books numerous Top Pick and Recommended Reads designations; her historical erotic romance *Tangled Past* was nominated as Best Erotic Menage of 2011 by The Romance Reviews in their Best Book of 2011 contest, and Leah received another CAPA nomination from The Romance Studio reviewers for *Deliberate Deceptions* as Best Contemporary Romance of 2011.

For more information about the Hauberk series, as well as her other books, visit her website at LeahBraemel.com. You can also follow Leah on Twitter at @LeahBraemel or find her on Facebook at facebook.com/AuthorLeahBraemel.

CPSIA information can be obtained at www.ICGtesting.com
Printed in the USA
LVOW081546221212

312900LV00003B/31/P